THE CHERRY VALLEY MIDDLE SCHOOL

DEAR KNOW-IT-ALL

★ ★ ★

Late Edition

WITHDRAWN

by RACHEL WISE

Simon Spotlight

New York London Toronto Sydney New Delhi

SIMON SPOTLIGHT
An imprint of Simon & Schuster
Children's Publishing Division
1230 Avenue of the Americas,
New York, New York 10020
Copyright © 2013 by Simon & Schuster,
Inc. All rights reserved, including the
right of reproduction in whole or in
part in any form.
SIMON SPOTLIGHT and colophon are
registered trademarks of
Simon & Schuster, Inc.
Text by Elizabeth Doyle Carey

For information about special discounts
for bulk purchases, please contact
Simon & Schuster Special Sales at
1-866-506-1949 or
business@simonandschuster.com.
Manufactured in the United States of
America 1213 OFF
First Edition 10 9 8 7 6 5 4 3 2 1
ISBN 978-1-4424-9724-5 (pbk)
ISBN 978-1-4424-9725-2 (hc)
ISBN 978-1-4424-9726-9 (eBook)
Library of Congress Control Number
2013951907

Chapter 1

SUBURBAN TEEN DIES OF SLEEP DEPRIVATION!

★ ★ ★

I rolled over and stared at the clock next to my bed. The numbers cast a bloodred glow across both the computer and the empty diet cola can on my bedside table. It was 1:05 a.m. I quickly did the math in my head for the tenth time that night: My alarm will go off at 6:15, which means if I fall asleep *right this very second*, I will still get only five hours and ten minutes of sleep.

Which is not enough.

I sighed heavily and flopped on my back to stare at the ceiling. I'd read an article a few months ago on Huffington Post about teenagers and how their internal clocks are out of whack with the rest of society. I guess a lot of studies have been done and teenagers' bodies need to stay up late and sleep late. (Like I did this morning. Blissful eleven-o'clock Sunday-morning sleep-in!) It's some kind of adaptation that has developed over thousands of years. Maybe I should pitch an article to Mr. Trigg, our school newspaper advisor, on teenage sleep patterns. That could be good. I flipped on my lamp, wincing at the brightness, and reached for my laptop to e-mail the idea to myself. (My trusty notebook was already packed in my messenger bag and I didn't feel like getting up to get it.) After closing the computer, I switched off the lamp and settled back under the covers with a sigh, waiting for sleep to come. I sighed again loudly and fluffed my pillow. Nothing.

Suburban Teen Dies of Sleep Deprivation!
I wondered how fast it could happen.

At some point I must've fallen asleep, but it was well after one thirty, because that was the last time I remember doing my sleep math.

★　　★　　★

"Sammy, sweetheart, you're going to be late if you don't get up right now!" My mom sounded stressed.

"Yeah, sweetheart!" sang out my sister, Allie, passing by my room—while texting, I'm sure.

I groaned and thought about how I keep meaning to wear clean school clothes to bed so all I have to do is roll out and brush my teeth. Tonight. For sure.

"Just put your feet on the floor. Once you're up and moving, it will be a whole lot better. I promise," said my mom, watching me with folded arms from her perch in the doorway.

I did as she said and mentally reviewed my day, trying to figure out the soonest moment I could get some shut-eye, even if it was just a nap in the library. But I have a newspaper meeting, I'm helping my BFF, Hailey Jones, with her English essay after school (she's a dyslexic math whiz, and I love to write and hate math—we are a perfect match), and I need to sneak by my mailbox in the newspaper office at some point to see if there are any letters for my column, Dear Know-It-All. I sighed heavily and stood up.

"Okay, Mom. I'm up and it's not better!" I called, but she had already left.

Allie walked by going the other way now, fully dressed, laughing into her phone.

"What kind of people talk on the phone at this hour of the day?" I grumbled under my breath.

And Allie, who never hears me when I speak directly to her, managed to catch my snide comment and threw back, "Busy people with lots of friends, that's who!"

I rolled my eyes and began to get dressed. "I have lots of friends!" I called back, but of course she didn't hear me.

★　　★　　★

My mom was a little bit right, in that once my day was under way, I wasn't as tired as I'd been all snuggled under my down comforter. Getting up in the morning is kind of like writing on deadline. You dread it, and it's hard to get started, but once you get going, everything just flows. That's how it is for me anyway. Maybe not for Hailey, though.

We were at lunch and Hailey was fake banging her head against the table.

"But *why* do we care what Mr. Rochester thinks?"

"It's the whole point of the book, Hailey," I replied, weary now of the argument and my day. "And I just know that's what Mr. Taylor is looking for in your essay on Jane Eyre."

Hailey looked forlornly into space. Then she sighed. "Okay. Okay, I'll do it. I guess."

I had to chuckle. "It's not like you have a choice, Hails. It's the assignment."

Hailey flashed a mischievous grin at me. "I can actually get out of certain assignments. Or I can do them differently if I want. It's part of my ISP."

ISP means Independent Study Plan, which Hailey gets because of her dyslexia. She also gets a tutor, but she prefers working with me so she cancels the tutor a lot.

"Hmm, maybe I should get an ISP so I can write an *essay* for the *math* exam!" I giggled.

Hailey's eyebrows went up at the suggestion. "Great idea! I can help you! Here's what you need to do. . . ."

"Kidding!" I said. "What I really need is an ISP to have my day start later. I can't get to sleep at night, and it's driving me crazy!"

"Why?" asked Hailey, picking up a glazed doughnut from her tray and chewing thoughtfully. Hailey's mom is a health nut so in Hailey she has created a junk-food nut.

"Well . . . it all started with midterms. I had two huge exams and an article, and—" Oops! I caught myself just as I was about to say "My column!" No one, and I mean no one (not even my best friend) knows that I am Dear Know-It-All! Just me, my mom, and the faculty advisor to the paper, Mr. Trigg. "And . . . I don't know, something else. But I stayed up late a bunch of nights in a row, and it was like my body got adjusted to this new time clock and then I couldn't reset it."

"Like suddenly you were living in the wrong time zone?" asked Hailey.

"Sort of." I shrugged. "I'm just wired at eleven o'clock at night, and I should be sacked out."

"Huh," said Hailey with a shrug. "I never have any sleep problems. I pass out at night and pop up at the same time every morning. I don't know why!"

"Well, you're lucky," I grouched.

"Who's lucky?" asked a husky voice over my shoulder.

My ears tingled. My heart raced. It was Michael Lawrence, the one true love of my life—peanut butter to my jelly, Mario to my Luigi, Romeo to my Juliet!

"Hey," I said coolly, revealing nothing of the drama going on inside my heart.

"Ready to go to the meeting?" he asked.

Hailey slumped in her seat and did a fake pout. "You're always stealing her from me!" she whined.

"Hey, I can't help it if I'm charming!" joked Michael.

"Duty calls," I said in a resigned voice, standing up and gathering my things.

"Duty?" said Michael, mock outraged.

Hailey and I exchanged a private smile. She knew there was nothing I'd rather do than hang out with Michael Lawrence, and she is pretty much okay with that.

A voice came from the other direction. "Hey,

Hails, cute shirt! Mind if I join you?"

I looked up. It was Molly Grant, a seventh grader I know a little. I felt immediately better. As much as Hailey doesn't mind me taking off, at least now I wouldn't be leaving her at the table all alone.

But Hailey jumped up. "Uh, sorry . . . ," she muttered. "We were just leaving."

As I walked away, I glanced back at Molly's face and saw she was hurt. I felt bad, but now I was in a bit of a rush and, anyway, it wasn't my problem. As Hailey fell into step next to me on our way to deposit our lunch trays, I said quietly, "What was that all about? Where do you need to be?"

Hailey huffed in exasperation. "That girl drives me nuts! There is no *way* I'm going to sit there with her while you leave."

"I think she seems nice," I said, because I do.

"Well, that's because she isn't constantly appearing next to you, wearing exactly what you wore yesterday."

I looked at Hailey in confusion. "What do you mean?"

"She copies me constantly! I wear red high-tops; she shows up the next day in brand-new red high-tops. I cut the sleeves off a T-shirt and layer it, and she does the same the next week. It's driving me insane!"

"Hmm. I don't blame you, but I can't really get into this now." I glanced at Michael, who was waiting in the cafeteria doorway. He was chatting with Kate Bigley, whom I always worry he secretly likes.

"More on this later. Gotta go. Sorry," I said.

"Okay, bye." Hailey sighed. "Good luck."

I smiled and raced off.

Chapter 2

DOUBLE LIFE EXHAUSTS JOURNALIST; SECRETS ARE WEARING HER DOWN

★ ★ ★

Michael and I arrived at the newspaper office with a few minutes to spare. We settled into our usual front-row spot on the low-slung love seat and waved hello to our colleagues as they arrived.

"Any ideas to pitch?" I asked Michael. I stretched and then gave a big yawn as I relaxed into the little couch.

"Nothing pressing," he said. "You?"

"I . . . oh . . ." I covered my gaping yawn with both hands. "I was thinking of pitching an article on kids and sleep."

"Looks like you could use some, Sleepy," he teased.

I rolled my eyes. Ever since Michael caught me tasting paste in kindergarten, he has called me "Pasty" or some variation on the "-y" nickname, like "Trippy" if I trip over something or "Snacky" if I'm hungry.

"Oh, shush, Mikey!" I growled back, using his family nickname as retaliation.

He grinned, his bright blue eyes twinkling and his dimples deepening. My heart fluttered even as I wanted to slap him.

"I'd work on that with you, if you want," he offered.

"Good," I said. "Let's see if Trigger likes it."

"How do you think the paper has been looking lately?" asked Michael, just making idle chitchat.

"Pretty good! I think we're hitting our stride for the year. The new kids are up to speed, the editor in chief seems to know what she's doing now, and I've liked a lot of the articles lately. What do you think?"

"I totally agree." Michael nodded. "It's looking

pretty tight. The only thing . . . well . . ." He paused, like he didn't want to say something.

"What? Is it me? Am I not doing well?"

"No! Oh no. Sorry. Not you. I was just thinking of Dear Know-It-All, whoever that is."

"Oh." I tried to play it really cool. "Yeah. Who *is* that?" I looked at him with what I hoped was a suspicious expression, as if I suspected it might be *him*. Michael looked back at me steadily. I always think he knows it's me, but then he'll do something that indicates otherwise. He continued. "I just think the Dear Know-It-All answers have been a little rushed lately. Like they've been shorter than usual and not as much fun to read, you know? Maybe not as much effort put into them."

I nodded, acting cool, while inside I was raging. *Do you think it's easy to come up with good questions from the piles of junk kids submit every week? Do you have any idea how hard it is to be diplomatic and not say anything the school wouldn't like, while still providing a meaty enough answer? I'd like to see you try to find the time to write this column and do a good job each issue,*

Mr. Smarty-Pants! Instead, I said, "Huh. Maybe you should tell Mr. Trigg so he can pass that on to whoever writes the column." Then I gulped. Luckily, Michael wasn't looking at me right then.

"Yeah, I've been meaning to," said Michael. "I just don't want to get old Know-It-All in trouble."

"Oh. Good point. Well . . . maybe put the word out to all the people you think are . . . the likely writers of it?" I said innocently.

"I am," said Michael, looking me square in the eye. I looked away uneasily.

"Good luck with that," I said quietly.

"Hello, my wonderful scribes!" trilled Mr. Trigg, entering the room in a rush, his briefcase on his arm and his trademark green-and-blue striped scarf floating out behind him. "I apologize for my delay! The new installment in the Churchill biography was released today, and I wanted to be the first on line at the bookstore to get it. I lined up at eight a.m. so I'd be there when they opened the doors! So exciting!" He opened his briefcase and withdrew an enormously thick book and waved it about by way of explanation. "I'll pass it 'round so everyone can take a look. Oh, how long I've been waiting for this day! It's like Christmas and my birthday all rolled into one!"

We all laughed. Mr. Trigg is obsessed with Winston Churchill and manages to work him into nearly every conversation. Lucky for us journalists, Churchill was a pretty inspiring guy.

"Mr. Trigg, how long was the line? At the bookstore?" called Jeff Perry, the newspaper's photographer and one of Michael's best friends.

"Er . . . The line? Well, the wait was quite tedious, I'll say, but well worth it!" Mr. Trigg laughed.

Evading a question in front of a roomful of budding journalists is never a good idea.

"What was the exact head count on the line, Mr. Trigg?" called Michael.

"Maybe we should call the bookstore? Get them as a source?" suggested Kate Bigley from across the room.

Mr. Trigg knew when he was being teased, and he has a great sense of humor. Shaking his head from side to side, he looked up from the table and put his hands in the air. "All right, all right. I suppose my enthusiasm was greater than that of many of my fellow Cherry Valley residents. Either that or the majority of Churchill fans are late sleepers. But you can never be too safe in these crowdlike situations."

"Was there *anyone* else on the line besides you, Mr. Trigg?" asked Michael, and everyone laughed.

Mr. Trigg sighed. "It grieves me, the state of intellectualism in this country, and I hope you will all grow up to do something about it."

"Answer the question!" called Jim Peavy, another writer, from across the room.

"You win. Alas, it was only I." Mr. Trigg hung his head, clasping his folded hands to his heart, and everyone burst into applause. "And in the words of my mentor, the great man himself, 'Solitary trees, if they grow at all, grow strong.' Now, let this meeting come to order!"

Everyone was charged up and grinning. It was a great way to start the meeting. We all felt like a team. Everyone felt smart and energized, and it really paid off. We were ready to work.

I pitched my article on sleep, and Trigger liked it. He wasn't sure there was enough meat on it for me and Michael to share it, and for a moment I panicked that we'd be separated. But he thought for a minute and then assigned us a sidebar box on general teen health tips and said we could do the two together. Phew.

When Mr. Trigg was going down his column list asking for feedback, he passed over Dear Know-It-All, and I nudged Michael, as if to say, "Speak up." But Michael shook his head, whispering, "I don't want to embarrass the columnist."

Well, that was thoughtful anyway, and at least I'd covered myself by suggesting he announce his concerns, or I think I did anyway. I can never be sure.

Double Life Exhausts Journalist; Secrets Are Wearing Her Down.

"In case it's you," I added under my breath, and Michael smiled and rolled his eyes.

After the meeting adjourned, Michael and I agreed to brainstorm and do a little Internet research on sleep, and then we'd get back together to work on it. I headed out the newspaper office door to earthonomics (aka science class), and when I glanced down the hall, I was lucky enough to spot Hailey up ahead in her trademark jean jacket with the red stripe down the back.

"Hails!" I called, but she didn't turn around. "Hailey! Hailey Jones!" Nothing. I was pretty sure she could hear me. I jogged down the hall to catch up. "Hailey?" I said.

But when the girl turned, it wasn't Hailey. It was Molly Grant, wearing an identical jacket.

"Oh! I'm so sorry! I thought you were Hailey!" I said, laughing as my face pinkened.

"You did?" gushed Molly. "Oh, what a compliment! Thank you so much!"

Okay, that was *so* not the reaction I was expecting. "Um . . . you're welcome?"

"You just made my day!" said Molly, and she continued happily on down the hall, leaving me standing there dumbfounded. I thought about Hailey and I cringed. She would not be happy when she heard about this.

In class, we got our tests back—the one I fell asleep studying for at midnight last week—and I got a C. It was such a bummer, I felt sick. It wasn't like I had tried my very best, because it would stink to get a C under those circumstances, but it was just that I knew I wouldn't have had the time to even *try* to do better.

Dr. Shenberg, the earthonomics teacher, said if anyone did badly on the test and wanted to improve their grade-point average, they could do a poster for the science fair and receive up to ten extra points for their grade. Obviously, I was one of the people that announcement was directed at, but when the heck was I going to find the time to do a science fair poster on top of everything else? *ACK!*

★   ★   ★

By the time the final bell rang that day, I was beat and stressed and I still had to pick up some DKIA letters, tutor Hailey, do my own homework, and start a little research for my article. Oh yeah, and think up a science fair poster topic.

I grabbed a soda from the vending machine

and chugged it, feeling the sugar surge almost immediately and praying for the caffeine to kick in. All I really wanted to do, though, was go home and take a nap.

I popped into the empty newspaper office, locked the door, and spirited my letters out of the DKIA mailbox without getting caught. Phew. Then I went out to meet Hailey at the bike rack.

"Okay, weird story for you," I said by way of greeting. Then I proceeded to tell Hailey about my interaction with Molly Grant in the hall.

Hailey banged her palm down on the handlebars of her bike as she walked it along. "You see? That's what I'm talking about! That girl copies every single thing I do! My haircut, my clothing, my bike, even the way I drew my name on my binder! It's so annoying!"

"Huh." *Quick! What would Dear Know-It-All say?* I wondered. "Well . . . you know my mom always says 'Imitation is the sincerest form of flattery.' It's a compliment. She looks up to you and wants to be just like you!"

Hailey scoffed. "My mom said that too, but it

really bugs me. Also because I do things and then she gets credit for them, like the way I drew on my sneakers, or how I put the air freshener in my gym locker, stuff like that. Then all the kids say, 'Oh, Molly! That's so cute!' or, 'Oh, Molly, you're so smart!' when it was *me* all along! Plus I am an individual. I don't like to think there's another one of me walking around, you know?"

"Yeah. Actually, I can really see how annoying it is." I tried to think of a solution. "Have you ever confronted her about it?" I asked.

"As if!" huffed Hailey. "Like, 'Hi, I'm so great and I know you copy me, so stop!' Can you picture that? I'd get a reputation as the vainest person at school!"

"Well, Molly's only in the seventh grade, so I doubt it would go much further than her class . . . ," I joked.

"Don't joke. It's not funny," ordered Hailey.

"Sorry."

"Maybe make yourself unlikable? Or do stuff that's so out there it will be obvious to everyone that she's copying you and maybe other people will call her out on it and she'll get embarrassed and stop?" I joked.

"Like what?" said Hailey in all seriousness.

"Hailey, I was kidding," I said.

"Seriously, it just might work. I'll brainstorm," said Hailey. She reached out to give me a sideways squeeze. "You always give the best advice!" she said, cheerful now. "I'm telling you, they picked the wrong person to write those Dear Know-It-All answers, whoever they are!"

I gulped and forced a smile onto my face. "Yeah!" I agreed heartily.

Best Friend Lies Continuously to Best Friend; Ulcers Inevitable.

Chapter 3

SISTERS GET LATE-NIGHT GIGGLES!

★ ★ ★

Hailey and I slumped around the house, ate some junk food, and got her homework done; then I ate a huge dinner, trying to keep my energy up. I finished my homework as quickly as possible and took a hot shower to stay awake for my extracurricular newspaper and science fair work.

I got into my pj's, brushed my teeth, grabbed my laptop, and got under the covers. I felt a little sick from how much I'd eaten—like I was overly full, but I ignored it and tried to get comfortable. My room was kind of hot, but I didn't want to get out of bed to go turn down the thermostat so I just dealt with it. I spent about an hour Googling possible science fair topics and hit on the topic of newspaper printing. There's some interesting stuff about inks and offset rollers and digital files, and I knew I could get a trip to the printers out of it with Mr. Trigg, so I could have some firsthand photos or flyers or whatever. It could be good. I'd just have to figure out when to fit it in.

At ten o'clock my mom called up the stairs, "Sammy! I'm coming up to say good night soon! If you're not ready for bed, make sure you get ready now because it's lights-out in ten minutes!"

"Okay!" I called back. I was ready for bed, but now I wasn't tired at all and I was just getting cracking on all this research. There was no way I could stop at this point. If she made me turn out my light, I could still Google stuff in the dark after she left, so I knew I'd better look at the new Dear Know-It-All letters while I still had my light.

I reached over to the folder behind my desk where I keep all my DKIA correspondence; I'd stowed today's new letters there earlier. There were only two, and I pulled them out and glanced at them; one was actually a postcard from Disney World, which was kind of funny. Mr. Trigg had already slit open the other letter and had read them both; he does that to protect me because I had a kook one time sending me hate mail.

The postcard said:

Dear Know-It-All,

I learn so much from real life. Why do I have to go to school? Seriously, what's wrong with just traveling the world and learning that way?

From,

The Wanderer

I smiled. It was a cute question, and I thought for a minute about whether it would make a good column. One rule of thumb I use in picking the letters is that if my answer will come out sounding like a parent, which I do not want, then I don't use that letter. I want to sound like a sympathetic friend, or maybe a smart older sister or brother, not someone who's lecturing the readers and sounding like a parent. But this one would be kind of like that.

I sighed and put it aside.

The second one was on nice pale green stationery with a little floral design on the back of the envelope and at the top of the sheet of paper when I took it out. It said:

Dear Know-It-All,

I think eighth grade is a lot harder than seventh. I can't deal with all the homework, extracurriculars, and projects. I'm not happy. I never have time to hang out with my friends anymore, plus I feel soooo stressed out all the time. What should I do?

Please help!

(signed)

Stressin' in the Valley

Wow. I could totally relate to this one. I sat back to think about what I would say in response and knew I could come up with something that didn't sound too lecture-y or adultish.

There was a knock on the door, and I wedged my computer between my sheets and jolted up in my bed to fumble the mail back into the folder in case it was Allie, the nosiest sister ever. But it was just my mom.

"Sam?"

Shoving the folder back behind the desk, I called, "Come in!"

My mom opened the door with a smile on her face. "Lots of fumbling around in here. Everything okay?" she asked, looking around the room suspiciously.

I let out a sigh of relief. "Yes. Just my . . ." and I mimed writing and mouthed, "Dear Know-It-All." My mom nodded and winked in understanding. She was in on Dear Know-It-All—the one person besides Mr. Trigg whom I could discuss it with—and it was often a relief to have her as a sounding board.

"Sleepy?" asked my mom, sitting down on the edge of my bed, closing my computer, and transferring it to the floor under my bedside table. She smoothed my hair back from my face.

I closed my eyes, then snapped them back open. "No," I said.

She laughed a little. "You just reminded me of yourself when you were a toddler. You went through this period where I could not get you to go down for the night. It was a nightmare! Then you'd be exhausted when I woke you up for day care the next morning, and you'd cry and cry."

"That's what I've been feeling like all week!"

She shook her head. "You poor thing."

"I just lie here and stare at the clock and count the hours all night long, all the while I'm getting more and more upset because I can't fall asleep! But then the next day I'm exhausted, and all I can think about is going back to bed. But then it happens all over again!" I punched my pillow hard and flopped it over.

My mom looked around my room. "Well, I see a can of soda there—which, by the way, no food or drinks outside the kitchen, please—is not helpful. What time did you drink that?"

"After school," I admitted.

"I'd avoid caffeine for a few days and see what

happens. I'm pretty sensitive to it, and you might be too."

"Okay," I agreed, but it was too late for tonight.

"Is everything else going okay?" asked my mom, her head cocked sympathetically.

I nodded. "Uh-huh. Just . . . it's a lot."

She looked at me in concern. "The schoolwork? The extracurriculars? The social life?"

"All of it," I admitted.

My mom sighed. "I love to see you having such a rich and busy life. You're so much more organized and motivated than I was at your age. But maybe I've pushed you too hard."

"No, it's not that, and you don't push me. I like it all, but it's just hard to fit everything in and . . . do it well," I added. Then I gulped and admitted, "Like, I got a C on the earthonomics test I got back today."

"Oh, Sammy! That's too bad. Did you study for it?"

I shrugged. "Kind of. I mean, I'm sure if I'd had more time I could have done better, but it was hard. And now I have to do an extra-credit project to make up the grade, and I just don't know when I'll find the time!"

"Maybe you should just accept the C on this test and resolve to get an A on the next one?" suggested my mom. "I don't want to see your world turning upside down over just one grade."

"No. Accepting the C seems kind of weak," I said.

My mom thought for a second and then she said, "Listen, sweetheart, if you need to take a break from the paper, or your column, or whatever, I'm sure Mr. Trigg would understand. I'd be happy to speak with him."

But then I'd never see Michael! "No. It's okay," I said. "Let me keep going for a while. I'll tell you if it is really too much."

"Pinkie promise?" asked my mom, crooking her little finger and holding it out to me. I crooked mine and we linked pinkies and wiggled them around. I giggled.

"Pinkie promise," I said.

"Okay then, lights out. And no more computer! I put your laptop under your bedside table, and I expect it to stay there. No exceptions!"

"Fine," I huffed.

She kissed me good night, pulled my covers up to my chin, turned out the light, and went to close the door. Just before she did, though, she said, "Maybe you could do the science project with a partner?"

As much as I wasn't really in the mood to accept her advice, it wasn't a bad idea. "Okay. I'll see. Maybe."

She blew me a kiss and left, while I settled in for what was sure to be a long night of ceiling staring.

About an hour later, I was so frustrated, my heart was racing. I couldn't sleep, and my anger at this fact was making me even more awake. I decided to get up and watch some TV.

Downstairs, I snuggled onto the sofa in the den and found a funny movie to watch. Wrapped in a cozy blanket and engrossed in the movie, I lost track of time. What felt like minutes later, the movie was ending, and suddenly Allie was at my side.

"Sam!" she whispered sharply. "What are you doing up?"

I nearly shrieked in surprise, I was so engrossed in the movie. "Allie!" I cried.

"Why aren't you in bed?" she demanded in a low voice.

"I couldn't sleep!" I protested. "Why aren't you in bed?"

"Same," Allie huffed. "Listen, why don't you try some hot milk with me? Watching teen flicks at two a.m. isn't exactly good for your biorhythms."

"Hot milk sounds gross."

Allie sighed, suddenly sympathetic, though I'll never know why. *(Scientist Cracks Code to Teen Mood Swings, Wins Nobel Prize!)* "I'll make some for you. It's supposed to really work."

We crept up to the kitchen, and Allie quietly filled a small saucepan with milk and heated it gently on the stove. Then she filled a mug and gave it to me with a small napkin. Sometimes she can be really nice. I'm not sure why.

"Thanks," I said, and I took a tentative sip with Allie watching.

"Well?"

"Well, what? Like is it good, or am I about to fall asleep right here at the table?"

Allie giggled. "Both."

I took another sip and tipped my head to the side to think. "It's not good, but it's not awful. It's kind of just milky and warm."

"That's because it's warm milk!" Allie laughed. "Are you tired yet?"

I thought again. "Maybe. Let me drink some more and I'll see." For some reason, this was really funny to us and we got laughing quietly but really hard. The quieter we tried to be, the funnier it was until we were in hysterics.

I took the last slurp of the milk and stood up to put the mug in the sink. "Well, that was the most fun I've had in weeks," I said to Allie, my eyes still watering from my tears of laughter.

"We'll have to do it again sometime," said Allie, and because we were in that dumb state of mind, we got laughing again.

Sisters Get Late-Night Giggles!

By the time I got into my bed, I really was

spent, and I conked right out, still smiling, I'm sure.

And though it wasn't a great night's sleep, even twelve hours wouldn't have helped; nothing could have prepared me for what I saw when I got to school the next morning.

Chapter 4

WRITER REJOICES AS CRUSH AND PAL BATTLE FOR HER TIME!

★ ★ ★

As I was opening my locker, I felt a tap on the shoulder. I stood and turned to see who it was. It took a second to register that it was Hailey because she had dyed her short, spiky blond hair bright, neon pink!

"Hailey!" I gasped. I could not believe my eyes.

"It's just temporary!" she protested quickly. "Does it look just awful? I think I made a huge mistake!"

"Um," I said.

Teen's Tongue Tied in Knots as Grooming Tragedy Unfolds!

"Oh gosh. I knew I shouldn't have done it. I was so mad about Molly Grant copying me all the time that I decided I'd do something so obvious that if she copied me, everyone would know and would call her out on it. But in trying to punish her, I think I punished myself!" she wailed quietly.

"Okay. First of all, I'm glad it's temporary. Second of all, what did your parents say?" Hailey's mom and dad are pretty mellow, but her mom is kind of a hippie and she doesn't like it when we use cosmetics or other chemicals on ourselves.

Hailey rolled her eyes. "Well, my mom actually thought it looked cool—she said it reminded her of herself in her 'punk rock phase' back in the eighties, a million years ago. But then she made me get the package so she could Google the ingredients; I'm sure I'll get an earful after school today. And my dad just laughed and rolled his eyes. My brothers tortured me, of course, calling me cotton candy. . . ."

I giggled, and Hailey smiled.

"But I think we could have predicted something like that would happen anyway. They'd torture me even if I won the Miss America Pageant."

Behind Hailey's back, everyone who walked

past us did a double take at the sight of her hair, and Jeff Perry called out, "Hey, Pinkie!" then snapped a photo when Hailey turned.

"I think you're going to have to brace yourself for the reactions," I said.

Hailey nodded miserably. "I know. I'm dreading getting through the day."

"Well, it's not a great look, but . . . it was brave of you, anyway!" I was trying to look on the bright side.

"Hey, want to have a sleepover on Friday night?" asked Hailey.

"Sure!" I said. We hadn't planned anything fun in a while.

"Good. I just need something to take my mind off this hair."

Suddenly, Molly Grant appeared at our side. "Hailey! Wow! Your hair looks amazing!" she gasped in awe. "I love it! Where did you have it done?" She was looking all around Hailey's head, trying to see every angle.

"In my bathroom!" snapped Hailey. She looked at me in frustration, like, *See what I have to live with?* Maybe it was a little annoying, I admit, but it wasn't like Molly was being mean or anything.

"Wow, Hailey. It looks so pretty. You look like a rock star or something. Pink is totally your color. You're so brave to take this step!"

"Well, I'm taking another step right now, and it's to language arts class, so . . . on your way!" Hailey gestured Molly along with a shooing motion.

Molly didn't even seem offended. "Okay, enjoy your great new look! Bye, Sam! Bye for now, Hailey!"

"Bye for always," muttered Hailey.

"Hailey," I chided her. "I know she's a little perky and maybe bold, but she clearly likes you and means well and thinks you're supercool."

Hailey rolled her eyes and scoffed. "She's a pill. But at least I finally hit on something she won't copy."

★   ★   ★

At lunch, Michael Lawrence was on line with me at the Organic Option table, so he joined me and Hailey for lunch (woo-hoo!). We talked a little about our article, and I admitted I hadn't had a chance to research teen sleep problems yet.

"She was very busy helping me with my homework," said Hailey, batting her eyes.

"Okay, Pinkalicious, but she needs some time to herself today so she can get going on this thing. Neither of us likes waiting until the bitter end and turning in subpar work!" joked Michael as he wagged his finger at Hailey.

Writer Rejoices as Crush and Pal Battle for Her Time!

I put my hands in the air. "I'll do it today. I promise! Right after I do my stupid proposal for my extra-credit science project." I sighed.

"Oh! You too?" said Michael, buttering a slice of bread.

I nodded. "Why, *you* have to do it?" I was surprised Michael would ever get a bad grade on anything. He's so smart and he has a photographic memory.

Michael nodded. "I got a D."

"*D?*" I was stunned. "Did you even show up?"

Michael smiled wryly. "I didn't know we had a test that day. I thought Dr. Shenberg was joking when he said to put our books away and take out a pencil. I don't know how I missed it; I thought it was the following day."

"That happens to me all the time," offered

Hailey, and we all laughed.

The wheels in my head started spinning. "Um . . . want to see if we could do the extra-credit project together?" I asked, thinking of my planned field trip to the printer. It would be much more fun with Michael along.

I was thrilled to see his eyes light up. "Yeah! That would be great! What are you thinking of doing it on?"

I explained my plan and my topic and the little bit of research I'd already done and how I thought we could take a field trip with Mr. Trigg and get some cool samples of the paper in different stages of printing.

"I love it. You're a genius, Pasty!"

I rolled my eyes at the nickname, but inside I was happy at the compliment.

"I tell her that all the time!" Hailey beamed.

"Then you're a genius too, Pinkie," teased Michael, and we all laughed.

★   ★   ★

After school, Michael and I went to see Dr. Shenberg to pitch him our idea, which he loved. He made us

promise to share the work equally and not divide
it up, as he wanted us both to have learned and
worked on every aspect of the project to keep the
grade fair. In my mind, I was jumping up and down
and hugging Dr. Shenberg, but outside I played it
cool as a cucumber.

When we left, I said, "Next stop, the newspaper office to make a plan with Trigger."

"Oh bummer! I have to go to football," said
Michael, uncomfortably shifting his backpack
from one shoulder to the other.

"Oh. Well, that's okay. I've got it. I'll just let
you know what Trigger says." I shrugged.

"But what about what Dr. Shenberg said about
doing everything together? Want to just wait until
tomorrow and I can go with you?"

I bit my lip. "No. I'd rather just get it over with
so I can plan out my time for the week. It's not
a big deal. Is there any day you can't go to the
printer?" I asked.

Michael filled me in on his schedule and then
he said, "This is huge, Pasty. I owe you a batch of
cinnamon buns for this one."

I waved my hand, like, *No problem.* "I've got it. Not that I'd ever turn down the famous Lawrence buns!" Instantly, I slapped my hand over my big mouth. My face turned purple, and as Michael laughed at my gaffe, I ran away.

★   ★   ★

By the time I reached the newspaper office, I had regained my composure a little, cringing only when I thought of the words "Lawrence," or "buns," which was about every thirty seconds.

Mr. Trigg was at his desk, luckily, and I accepted a cup of his (noncaffeinated) tea, which is always on offer there, and settled in for a chat.

"Mr. Trigg, first of all, do you think the DKIA column is slipping?"

"Slipping? Oh no, my dear girl. It's quite good."

"Well, another journalist on the paper told me they didn't think the writing had been up to par lately. That it seemed rushed and not as thorough." I winced, remembering Michael's words.

Mr. Trigg cupped his chin in his hand and tapped his upper lip, which he always does when he's thinking. "Well, perhaps," he admitted. "But I also think the questions haven't been great. Maybe we'll devote you a little more space this time and you can write something longer."

Inwardly, I groaned. More work. Less sleep. And on it goes.

"Oh, and here's the latest." He handed me a file and I glanced inside, seeing just one letter. Just at that moment his phone rang and he gestured that I could go ahead and read it, so I shut his office door halfway and then stood there reading the letter. It said:

Dear Know-It-All,

I am so stressed out, yo. There's too much work at this place. I can't find the time to do anything else.

Signed,

Help

I folded it up and put it back in the file right as Mr. Trigg hung up. "It's a theme," he said.

I nodded. "I'll do the first one. It's better written. I need to think about my response though. I'll work on it tomorrow."

"Good thinking, Ms. Martone. Let me know if I can be helpful."

"Okay, thanks."

"Also, Ms. Martone, you must always be on your toes for professional envy. Oftentimes journalists will skewer each other's work for reasons more complicated than you'd think."

I thought of Michael and that just didn't fit.

Mr. Trigg continued. "So how's the article coming along on sleep?"

"Oh, just . . . ducky!" I said, using one of his words and giggling at it.

He smiled. "Excellent. And what else?"

"Actually, I need to ask you a favor. I've got to do a project for extra credit, for earthonomics. Actually, so does Michael Lawrence. And we were thinking of doing it on modern printing techniques and the process of printing a newspaper."

"Wonderful idea!" said Mr. Trigg, sipping at his tea.

"Thanks. And we were wondering if we could go with you on a print run one night?"

"Splendid idea! Absolutely! I'm going this Thursday night, and I'd love you two to tag along. It's quite interesting."

"Thanks!" I said. "It sounds great."

"Certainly. It's a plan. Have your parents bring you two here at nine p.m., and I will return you home afterward. It's quite a late-night event, I'm afraid, so do have your mother call me to discuss the details. You won't be home until after midnight."

"Oh," I said. "Well . . . I'm not usually asleep until after that anyway."

"You're not? That's awful! Growing children need plenty of sleep. Is that why you wanted to do the article on it?"

I nodded miserably.

"Well, do get to work so you can put any new practices to use immediately. I am sorry for the planned later night. It's just that is when we're slotted to be there. I can give you some of my sleep tips, though, for when I have my late Thursdays every other week. Would you like to hear them?"

"Okay," I said.

"Right. First of all, get everything done ahead of time. Homework, dinner, laying out your pajamas and socks. You don't want to have to do anything when you get home except take a warm—not hot—shower and have a light snack, like some crackers. Keep your house as dark as possible; don't use the bathroom light. Just keep the hall light on and shower in the dimness. It helps. If I think of anything else special I do, I'll let you know."

"Thanks. But one question: why the socks?"

Mr. Trigg laughed. "I don't rightly know. It's something my grandmother used to make us do when I was a boy, and I've always done it since!"

"Well, anything's worth a try!" I agreed.

"That's the spirit!" cheered Mr. Trigg.

I stood and gave him back my mug. "Thanks, Mr. Trigg. See you Thursday."

"Looking forward to it, Ms. Martone."

Chapter 5

STOP THE PRESSES! JOURNOS GO ON DATE TO PRINTER!

★ ★ ★

Most people wouldn't bother primping for a trip to a factory, but then most people wouldn't be going to a factory with the crush of their life! Thursday couldn't come fast enough, and I used all my nervous energy in the day in between to research printing techniques so I'd know what questions to ask on the tour.

I Googled a lot and even called two factories with questions. I examined different newspapers and looked up where they were printed. I made a plan to meet with Michael on Friday after school (I am so bold!) to go over my findings, but in the meantime I'd sketched out a flow chart I thought we could use for a poster.

Meanwhile, Hailey had a big English paper due, so I helped her with that on Wednesday. I then had to stay up pretty late to finish my homework, but now I was thinking of myself as "in training" for Thursday's late night so I decided I'd just let it ride. I went back to my old friend caffeine and slugged down a couple of colas both Wednesday and Thursday to keep my eyes open. (It mostly made me feel sick.)

By Thursday evening at six thirty, I'd finished my homework (not my best effort), showered, dressed in a cute outfit, laid out my pj's and some socks for when I got home, and I was just beginning to noodle around on the sleep article. The only problem was whenever I researched sleep, it made me tired! I was basically nodding off in front of my laptop when my mom came into my room and busted me.

"Samantha, you are exhausted! Why don't you postpone this trip for another week and just go to bed?"

My head snapped up and my eyes flew open. "Was I asleep?"

"Practically! Oh, sweetie, this is too much! You have dark circles under your eyes! I'm thinking I might just forbid you from going tonight. . . ." She bit her lip.

"No!" I wailed, being careful not to burst into tears because a) it would ruin the tiny amount of mascara I had put on and b) whenever Allie and I cry for no good reason, my mom says we're overtired. The last thing I needed right now was to confirm her plans to keep me home. So instead I took a deep breath and said in a very calm voice, "I've got to get this project done this weekend so I have time to write my article and my"—I lowered my voice to a whisper—"*column*. . . . Plus it's all set up and Mr. Trigg is excited and Michael . . ."

My mom folded her arms and narrowed her eyes, assessing me. "You need to think about yourself, Samantha Martone."

I sighed heavily. "Fine. *I* want to go."

Mother/Daughter Staring Contest Ends in Draw.

Finally my mom sighed and said, "All right. But a new sleep plan is going into effect very soon." And she turned on her heel and left.

"Phew," I muttered. Then I shook my head a little to stay awake. Getting back to my laptop, I searched "Teen Sleep Habits" and found over 1.8 million results! I looked at my watch. We had to leave in fifteen minutes, so I had a little time. I started reading through the articles and taking notes. What I found was surprising and kind of scary.

For instance, teen drivers who are measurably tired are as compromised in their driving skills as drunk drivers! Sleep deprivation can also make you break out, get sick, become dependent on drugs, and do badly in school. Yuck. The more I read, the more stressed I got! I started jotting down notes and quickly filled a page. This was going to be a great article for us!

The fifteen minutes flew, and my mom was soon back in the door to get me for my ride to school to meet Mr. Trigg and Michael. I couldn't wait!

On the way there, she gave me a stern lecture about putting myself first and how I shouldn't feel obligated to help my friends when it was at my own expense and how I had to be careful not to bite off more than I could chew. I could see her point a little.

"Sam, you need to prioritize yourself. I know you are a wonderful and generous person who also likes to have a good time. But it's no fun being the one who's up all night working because you've spent all day helping others or playing."

I sighed in annoyance, but I admitted that she kind of had a point in theory, though it was hard to say no in practice.

"Okay, Sam, then let's practice for a minute. Pretend I'm Hailey and turn me down. Ready? Hey, Sam, can I come over after school so you can help me with my paper?"

I rolled my eyes. "No."

"Pretty pleeeease?" whined my mom, sounding scarily like Hailey.

I giggled. "No."

"I'll be your best friend."

"No!" I said firmly.

"Fine, then we're not friends anymore!"

"Mom!"

"Why are you calling me mom?" said my mom.

"Stop! Okay, I get the point!" I shouted.

My mom grinned and looked over at me. "Hailey has a tutor that is paid for by the state. I love that you're a good friend to her, but you are not obligated to help her with her homework. As of today, you are taking two weeks off."

"Mom! I can't do that! Hailey's final draft is due Monday!"

My mom looked over at me again, her mouth set in a firm line that meant business.

I slumped in my seat. "Fine," I said in a small voice. "But she's not going to like it."

"And the same goes for Michael Lawrence," said my mom, as she turned into the school parking lot. "Now we've run out of time, but I just want to say, you don't have to do more than your share of the work just so he'll like you. He already does like you."

"What-*ever*, Mom," I said, gathering my messenger bag, which had my notebook and my printouts from searching "Newspaper printing process" on the Web.

"Samantha, just remember. If you give away all of your feathers, you'll have nothing left to line your own nest."

"Ohhh-kay! Bye, Mom."

"Bye, sweetheart. Have fun."

I shut the door firmly, restraining myself from slamming it. Why did my mom have to be so nosy all the time? Heading up the walk toward the front door, I saw headlights pull in behind me. It was Michael's dad's SUV. I paused to wait for him as he said good-bye to his dad and caught up. Michael looked like he might have made a little extra effort to get spiffed up for tonight too. His hair was freshly washed and still damp, neatly parted and combed, and he had on clean clothes—a button-down and fresh cords—plus Top-Siders instead of his usual sneakers. I felt butterflies in my stomach, hoping he'd dressed up for me.

Stop the Presses! Journos Go On Date to Printer!

"Hey," he said.

"Hey," I answered with a dopey grin. He smiled back.

Mr. Lawrence tooted the horn, and we turned to wave and then headed in to find Mr. Trigg in the newsroom.

"How's the workload?" asked Michael.

I groaned. "Awful. I mean, I've finished everything that's actually due tomorrow, but the long-term stuff and the news article . . . and the research for the science project . . ."

"Wait! You're not supposed to be doing science project research without me!" protested Michael, the anguish plain on his face. "We agreed! I thought we were supposed to do it tomorrow after school!"

"I . . . uh . . . well . . . I just thought . . ."

"Come on, Sam. I mean, I know you're a perfectionist, but this could really get me in trouble. If you do all the work, how can I take the grade for it?"

The last thing I'd expected was for Michael to get mad that I'd worked ahead on our project. It made *me* mad.

"Hey, I'm doing you a favor, buddy! And I can't pull things off last-minute like you can! I need to work a little day by day and then put it all together. I'm not some . . . Last-Minute Lucy!"

Michael laughed, which was a relief. "Last-Minute Lucy?" he teased. Well . . . sometimes you are, actually," he said.

"Well, I don't like it when I am," I protested.

"Tomorrow, when we meet, we are going to divide this work up evenly, even if it might mean we can't use some of your research. Deal?"

This was really annoying. "Maybe."

Michael stopped in his tracks and folded his arms. "If you don't agree, I'm calling my dad to come back and get me and you can do this project alone."

I huffed in annoyance. "Fine, I guess."

"Good. And thank you, but don't try to do me any more favors. Now, let's hurry or we're going to be late."

We scurried to the newsroom, where Mr. Trigg was just shutting off the lights.

"Cheers!" he called as we piled in through the doorway.

"Hi, Mr. Trigg!" I said.

"Almost ready! Just one last thing . . ." He ducked into his office and came out with three big sets of earphones, the kind air-traffic controllers wear.

I laughed. "What are those for?"

Mr. Trigg looked at me in surprise. "Have you ever been to a factory before?"

I shook my head.

"Then you shall see!"

It took about half an hour to get to the factory in Mr. Trigg's car. At times, I'd close my eyes and pretend that Michael and I were on a date and that Mr. Trigg was his dad, driving us to the movies or something. I even caught myself smiling at one point and had to quickly look out the window so that Michael wouldn't see me.

After a half hour's drive, we ended up in an industrial park in Newark that said "FlyPrint" across the side of the building in huge letters. There were big trucks from all the major national newspapers lined up outside, waiting with their engines idling.

"Whoa! They print the *New York Times* here?"

I asked in awe. The *New York Times* is like the ultimate, as far as I'm concerned. It would be my dream to one day write for them.

Mr. Trigg nodded. "Not in the same area as the *Cherry Valley Voice*, of course, but it's the same company. First, we will be touring the big plant, where they print the big boys; the *Voice* is printed in a small annex off to one end. Not nearly as glamorous!" He pulled the car into a parking spot and we all got out. Mr. Trigg pulled his earphones around his neck into a ready position and handed ours to us to do the same.

"Follow me!" he said, clapping his hands in excitement. "Oh, how I love the smell of freshly printed newsprint!"

Michael and I exchanged a look and laughed. We were excited too.

The lobby of FlyPrint could have been any corporate lobby. The receptionist greeted Mr. Trigg by name and told us to go on in, that Jack Dunleavy was waiting for us.

"Jolly good! Thank you!" said Mr. Trigg. He ushered us down a long hall, around a corner,

and toward a huge door. I could hear a din from
behind the door and knew that must be the factory area, but before we went in, Mr. Trigg took
a quick right into an office. We followed him.
Inside was a conference table surrounded by
cushy leather chairs, a TV on the wall showing
CNN, vending machines, and a huge plate-glass
window that looked out on the massive factory
beyond. Sitting on one of those cushy chairs was
a middle-aged man with a big belly. He was wearing a short-sleeved shirt, a tie, and suit pants and
was watching TV. He popped up when we came
in, and Mr. Trigg introduced us all around.

Mr. Dunleavy explained that he was the
Cherry Valley Voice's sales rep and would be
touring us around, then returning us to the
conference room to watch a short, twenty-
minute film about the printing process while
he and Mr. Trigg did a print check for our
next issue. He said he'd be happy to answer
our questions as we went along, but since it
would be so noisy, we could also do a Q and
A after the film was over. I told him I had lots

of questions and would appreciate doing an interview with him, and he agreed.

Next, Mr. Dunleavy gave us a quick overview of the plant and what we were going to see. Fly-Print's main machine cost more than forty million dollars and was three stories high. It could print up to forty-eight thousand copies of a newspaper an hour. He described the process of receiving the digital files for the paper from a newspaper's editorial and production departments, preparing the printing plates and ordering the right amount of plain newsprint and ink for that day's edition of the paper, and he talked about how gentle the machines need to be because newsprint is very soft and thin and a damaged roll of paper loses thousands of dollars for the printer.

It all sounded so cool. I couldn't wait to get started.

An exciting thought popped into my mind just then. "Mr. Dunleavy, does working here mean you get to read tomorrow's news today?" I asked.

He smiled a wide, happy grin. "Yes, it does!"

"Wow," I said. "That is so cool."

He seemed pretty psyched that we were so into it and also that we'd picked this topic as an extra-credit project.

We put on our earphones and followed him in. Inside, we were assaulted by the din. It was like a freight train was running next to us, and Mr. Dunleavy had to shout to be heard. There were forklifts driving around with massive rolls of newsprint. (They looked like giant toilet paper rolls and weighed fifteen hundred pounds each!) We had to keep our hands in our pockets and our wits about us so we didn't get hurt. Unfortunately, this meant I couldn't take any notes; nor could we take any photos. Thank goodness for Michael's photographic memory.

When we got to the big roller where the front page of tomorrow's *New York Times* was being printed, I turned my head upside down to see if I could read the headline as it flew past, but the machine was too fast.

"No wonder it's called FlyPrint!" I yelled. Mr. Dunleavy laughed.

The tour lasted about twenty-five minutes.

Then we headed back to the conference room. The first thing I did was grab my notebook and start jotting down facts and figures and confirming what I remembered Mr. Dunleavy saying on the tour. I also noted some more questions I'd have for him after the film.

"We should do a story about this for the *Voice*, too," I said to Mr. Trigg and Michael as Mr. Dunleavy fiddled with the DVD and the TV settings.

Mr. Trigg nodded. "You can prepare it and we'll hold it on file to fill a slot," he suggested. That's never what a journalist wants to hear about her article (you want everything to be urgent, front-page news), but it's not like it would be hard to write this up after we finished the science project. Lots of journalists write file articles so the paper has things to run on slow news days.

Finally Mr. Dunleavy started the film on the TV and dimmed the lights.

"You never stop, do you?" said Michael quietly as Mr. Dunleavy and Mr. Trigg headed out for their print check, discussing a new improvement on the *Voice*'s printing line. I looked at Miguel curiously.

"Is that a good thing or a bad thing?" I asked.

Michael laughed. "Both. I just don't know when you find the time for it all," he said, shaking his head.

"Well, the same could be said about you!"

"I *don't* find the time! That's why I'm getting a D in science!" he protested.

"Well . . . I practically am, too," I said.

Michael rolled his eyes. "Not for long, though."

Michael and I settled into the cushy leather chairs in the dim, cozy conference room with the din of the printer wooshing right beyond the window. The credits rolled and then the film began with an exterior shot of the big FlyPrint words on the side of the building.

And that was the last thing I remember.

Chapter 6

WRITER FIRES PARTNER AT PRINTING PRESS SHOWDOWN!

★ ★ ★

"Samantha!"

Someone was gently poking my shoulder.

"Samantha! Ms. Martone!"

I sat bolt upright, with absolutely no idea where I was. I looked around in confusion: TV, conference table, vending machines . . . OMG! I fell asleep at the printer! I looked up and saw Mr. Trigg peering down at me. I jumped to my feet.

Mr. Dunleavy was laughing. "Yes, our film has that effect on some viewers."

"Oh, Mr. Trigg, I am so sorry. I'm so embarrassed. I can't believe I . . . Hey! Where's Michael?" I had just realized he wasn't in the room with us.

"Men's room," said Mr. Trigg.

"You woke him up first?" I asked.

Mr. Trigg shook his head and smiled. "He didn't fall asleep."

"Wait . . . it was just me?"

Mr. Trigg shrugged. "He said you'd been burning the candle at both ends and he'd taken notes for the both of you."

Michael walked in right then and with a gorgeous smile said, "Hey, Sleepy!"

It enraged me. "Michael! I can't believe you! How could you let me sleep like that?"

Michael raised his eyebrows and gestured toward Mr. Trigg and Mr. Dunleavy, which put my anger temporarily on hold. "I'm sorry," I said, reining myself in and turning to the two men to apologize. "I'm also sorry I fell asleep and missed the movie." I stared daggers at Michael as I said this.

Writer Fires Partner at Printing Press Showdown!

Mr. Dunleavy laughed again. "It's no problem. It *is* a late night for you kids. I can send you a link to it and you can watch it on our website in the comfort of your own home, if you like."

"Thanks. That's really nice. But now it's time to go and I still have so many questions for you!" Boy, I'd really made a mess of all this. I couldn't believe I'd fallen asleep at the printer! Ugh! So much for my big "date"!

"I'm sure you could chat by phone this week," said Mr. Trigg.

Mr. Dunleavy kindly agreed and handed us both his business card. He said it was a kick for him to see kids our age taking an interest in print when supposedly all our generation cared about was electronics, and he looked forward to chatting with us later this week.

Without further ado, we thanked him profusely and headed out to the car, by which time it was ten thirty, earlier than Mr. Trigg originally thought, but still past my official bedtime of ten o'clock.

In the backseat of the car, I rested my head against the headrest. I was mortified and crushed; I'd ended a really good experience on a bad note. It was very unprofessional to fall asleep in a situation like that, and I really was mad that Michael hadn't woken me up.

Mr. Trigg looked at me in the rearview mirror. "Feel free to take a snooze, Ms. Martone. Mr. Lawrence and I can wake you up when we reach your address."

I snapped my head up. "I'm fine. Thanks," I said sharply.

"*Riiiight*," said Michael Traitor Lawrence in a teasing tone of voice. I saw him and Mr. Trigg exchange a grin in the mirror.

"Looks like that sleep article is well timed, Ms. Martone," said Mr. Trigg.

"Humph," I said quietly, looking out the window.

"We'll be working on it all afternoon tomorrow," said Michael. "Just don't conk out on me, Sleepy." He chuckled.

And do you want to know the worst part? I fell asleep again! Try as I might, I could not keep my eyes open for the rest of the ride. Before I knew it, I had dozed off again and we were pulling up in front of my house.

"Ms. Martone, do remember the tips I told you for getting off to sleep tonight: socks, dim lighting, crackers. It all helps."

I nodded, too tired to chat. "Thank you *so* much Mr. Trigg. That was great. I can't wait to call Mr. Dunleavy and to write about it," I said. "See ya, Michael." I knew it was kind of a cool farewell, but I was still annoyed at him for letting me fall asleep in a professional setting. It made him look good and me look bad.

"Bye, Sleepy," he singsonged in an annoying voice. Had I *ever* liked him? I closed the car door (a bit firmly) and went inside.

My mom had waited up. "Samantha, you look exhausted. Was it great? Was it worth it?"

I nodded and managed a weary smile. "I'll tell you all about it in the morning." It was already eleven fifteen. Skipping a second shower, I went straight to put on my pj's and brushed my teeth in the dark; then I pulled on some socks and conked out, sleeping until my mom woke me up the next morning.

★   ★   ★

I was groggy still when I got to school, and I wasn't in a very good mood. I flashed back to my sleep research from the previous evening and remembered that lack of sleep causes "dysmorphia" or "bad mood" in kids. I had that now. Plus I was dreading working with Michael this afternoon because I was tired and still annoyed with him. All I wanted was to go home and watch TV in my pj's.

But at my locker, Hailey accosted me. "OMG. I am going berserk. Wait until you see. Just *wait* until you see."

"What's the matter, Hails?" I asked without a whole lot of enthusiasm.

"What's the matter? What's the matter? I'll tell you what's the matter. The matter is that that little . . . *troll* . . . Molly Grant . . . has dyed her hair pink! That is exactly what is the matter."

I slammed my locker door shut in shock. "No way!" I yelled.

I could tell Hailey was pleased by my reaction. She grinned and shook her head from side to side.

"Way! No kidding. The girl is out of control."

I slumped against my locker door, my mouth agape as I processed the news. "Wow. She didn't even wait a whole week!"

"I know!" said Hailey. "So before we do my paper this afternoon, I need your help in getting this gross stuff out of my hair once and for all."

I looked at Hailey. "Um," I said.

"What?"

"Um."

"What?"

"I can't do today, Hails. I'm so sorry."

"What do you mean you can't 'do' today?" she demanded. "My paper is due Monday! And now I've got to deal with this hair. I figured if Allie's home, she can help us."

I winced and thought of my practice session with my mom last night.

"No." I finally squeezed it out.

"Just no?" said Hailey.

I shook my head the tiniest bit and squeezed my eyes shut so I wouldn't have to see the look on Hailey's face.

"Oh fine. Whatever," she huffed. "I can call the tutor for the paper. They owe me like seven sessions anyway. But the *hair!*" she wailed. "And what about tonight?"

I opened my eyes. Had it really been that easy to say no to helping Hailey? I'd expected a big, huge drama and this was nothing. Now, in my relief, I felt grateful and generous. "We're still on for tonight. Meanwhile, do you want me to text Allie to see if you can stop by and have her help you?" Hailey worships Allie and Allie *does* kind of love it. I was willing to bet that if Allie was free, she'd help.

"Oh, Sammy, would you?" said Hailey, hanging on my arm in gratitude. I nodded, the generous benefactor, and dashed off a text to my sister.

"I'll let you know what she says," I said.

"Thanks," said Hailey.

Journalist Brokers Peace Accord; All Is Well.

We gathered our stuff and headed off to our classes. "So why can't you do it today?" asked Hailey.

I explained about the science project and the sleep article and admitted I had a meeting with Michael. "But it's business, not pleasure," I assured her.

"Or a little of both," she said with a small smile.

"No, trust me. It's business," I corrected her.

"Riiiight," said Hailey with an annoying smirk. She elbowed me and laughed, and right then, Molly Grant stepped out of the girls' bathroom. Her hair was flaming pink. It was such an obvious copy that she and Hailey looked like twins standing next to each other. Except for one thing.

Molly's eyes were red and swollen from crying.

She tried to brush past us without saying anything, but Hailey was still so mad she wasn't about to let her go without a fight.

"Hey, copycat. How do you like my hair now that you have it?" singsonged Hailey.

I gave Hailey a stern look; she can be a little *too* feisty sometimes.

Molly froze in her tracks but didn't turn around.

I glared at Hailey and then went to Molly's side and put my hand on her shoulder. "Hey, are you okay?" I asked quietly.

Molly began sobbing. "Everyone's . . . making fun of me and calling me Xerox. The people who don't know Hailey just"—*sob*—"think I look weird. And the people who do"—*sob*—"are mad at me for copying her. Everyone's being so mean!" she wailed. Then she put her hands up and covered her eyes and began to cry in earnest, like a little kid. I glanced at Hailey. Her mean smirk had faded to a look of concern. Hailey could be tough, but she wasn't psycho. She never wanted to see anyone upset like this.

"Okay, let's go back in the ladies' room," I said, wheeling Molly into an about-face.

From behind her hands Molly said, "Are you two going to beat me up in there? I don't even care. . . ."

"Beat you up? Are you nuts? We're going to help you get cleaned up!" said Hailey.

"Come on. We've got only three minutes until the bell rings," I said.

Inside the ladies' room, we propped Molly up

on the windowsill and got paper towels soaked with freezing-cold water and began to blot her face. Hailey looked in her knapsack and took out a baseball cap. "Put this on," she instructed. With a black baseball cap hiding most of her pink hair, Molly actually looked kind of cute. Still, we had to talk about the copying.

"Listen, Molly, the pink hair look doesn't work for anyone," I began.

"Thanks a lot!" said Hailey indignantly, but I silenced her with a glare.

"Maybe a little streak of it is fun now and then, but entirely pink is weird. That's number one. Number two is, you've got to lay off copying Hailey for a little while—"

"But I . . . ," interrupted Molly.

"Shssh. Listen to me. It's annoying to her, and everyone knows what you're doing. You need to be yourself. Find your own way. Do you understand?"

Molly sat there miserably. "I guess. But I just . . . I think you're the coolest!" she said to Hailey.

Hailey rolled her eyes and looked away to the side, but I could tell she was also secretly pleased. "Oh, what-*ever!*" she said.

I smiled. "Why don't you try to copy someone else for a while? Spread the love around, you know? Then Hailey won't feel so stalked."

"Yeah, like copy Sam here!" said Hailey.

Molly managed a weak smile.

"No, don't," I said. "Look, most people are copying someone, a little. Except maybe Lady Gaga. But you just need to mix it up—borrow a tiny idea from each person you admire—and then also make sure there's enough Molly in what you're doing too. Okay?"

The bell rang.

Molly took a deep breath. "Okay. I'll try."

"Don't try, *do!*" commanded Hailey. We all laughed.

"Thanks, you guys. I . . . I knew you were cool, but I didn't know you were nice, too," said Molly shyly.

"I'm not nice," said Hailey, but I elbowed her. Hard.

"Ow!" said Hailey.

"Thanks," I said to Molly.

My phone buzzed.

S— Tell H. meet me our house 3:00. —A

"You're good!" I told Hailey, and showed her Allie's text.

"Woo-hoo!" she whooped. "Maybe I should bring Molly and we'll get a group discount!"

"Please don't," I said. All I need is someone else copying Allie and her getting an even bigger head.

"I'll do the hair and then go home and get my stuff and come back for the sleepover. Pizza and the mall sound good?" she asked.

"Just what the doctor ordered!" I said.

Chapter 7

JOURNALIST OVERWHELMED BY ANGER, EMBARRASSMENT, AND LOVE, NOT NECESSARILY IN THAT ORDER

★ ★ ★

After school I met Michael outside by the bike rack. I was feeling a little testy still, since he'd let me fall asleep at the printer last night, so when he started off by calling, "Hey, Pasty!" in front of about five other kids, I scowled.

"Something wrong, Cranky?" he asked when I drew closer.

"The nickname thing is getting a little tired," I said.

"One day when we're old and gray, we will look back on it and laugh," he said.

That perked me up a little. Was he planning on growing old with me? Or maybe he just meant we'll be in the same nursing home or something. Ugh. I decided to make a little joke out of it since I didn't know what else to do.

"Right, and I'll call you Drooly," I said without cracking a grin.

"Thanks a lot!" he said with a big laugh. That reaction cheered me a tiny bit more out of my annoyance.

We began walking to Michael's house, which was on the other side of school from mine, but about the same distance.

I thought about my mom's pep talk last night and decided to say something to Michael to stick up for myself—at least to put it out there. So I said, "Uh . . . listen. I just want you to know . . . I was pretty ticked off that you left me sleeping last night at the printer."

I couldn't meet his eye, but I was glad I said it. I braced myself for his reaction.

There was a long pause. I glanced over to see why he hadn't said anything. Michael was looking up at the treetops as if struggling to find the right words to say. This was a first, so I was intrigued.

Finally he said, "I'm sorry, Sam. There were a lot of reasons I let you keep sleeping. I've been thinking about it since then and I feel really bad. It was selfish."

Now I was fired up. "You made me look like a slacker in front of two people whose opinions I care about and need!"

Michael blushed. "I just . . . You've seemed so tired lately, and I felt bad for you. And I . . . I guess seeing you sleeping there . . . I was sort of flattered that you felt comfortable enough to fall asleep in front of me. And . . . aaack!" Michael made a sound of frustration and stopped walking.

"What?" I asked, stopping too. Why were we stopping? Boys are so confusing.

Michael continued on awkwardly. "I . . . I guess part of me did feel superior, staying awake. And I didn't mind that Mr. Trigg and Mr. Dunleavy would see that."

"You see?" I practically shouted. "I knew it! I just knew you were trying to make yourself look good in front of them. And at my expense! That is so annoying!" I started turning around to leave right then and there. The nerve of this guy!

"Wait!" said Michael. He put his hand on my arm to stop me. "There was something else. More than the other stuff."

He took a deep breath and jammed his hands in his pockets. My arm still felt warm from his palm.

"This better be good," I said, tapping my foot on the sidewalk.

"Oh boy." Michael reached up and covered his face for a minute with both hands. When he took them away, he looked embarrassed. He took a deep breath. I did not know where he was going with this.

"I . . . You . . . you just looked so cute, asleep with your head on your folded arms, like a little kid. And it was so cozy in the room, and I felt like I was watching over you and it felt . . . good. I know that's so weird and dumb, but anyway, that's

why. That's why I didn't wake you up. That's all."
Michael looked away.

Um. Okay. Now it was my turn to blush, and
I looked away. I didn't know what to say. Nearby,
a little girl was holding her mom's hand, crossing the street to go to the park with her scooter.
We both watched for a minute until Michael spoke
again. "I'm sorry, Sam. You can go now. I just had
to say that because I didn't want you to think it
was just me being mean or trying to make myself
look better than you. That's all."

I cleared my throat, but my voice still came out
a little croaky. "Okay. Well. Right. Um. I'm . . .
glad you told me. And thanks? I guess? So. Just
don't ever get a job doing wake-up calls at a hotel,
okay? 'Cause you'll get fired."

It was a lame joke, but it broke the ice. Michael
laughed a little and shook his head. "Okay. I won't
ever get that job. I promise."

"Good," I said.

We both stood there awkwardly, each of us
looking off in a different direction. And finally
Michael said, "So, I guess you probably don't

want to do the project with me anymore, and I totally understand. Since it was your idea, it can be yours. I'll think of something else."

"No, it's fine. Really. I don't mind. We can be partners. On the project, you know. I mean." *Ugh, Martone!* I thought. *Why am I always saying inappropriate stuff?*

"And we still have the article," he said.

"Yeah . . . ," I said.

"Listen, Pasty, let's just forget about all this stuff and you can come over and we can work on our article and the project, okay? Friends?" Michael put out his hand for a shake.

With a sigh of relief, I agreed. "Sure. Friends." And we shook hands. "Good thinking. Let's get this over with," I said.

"Thanks a lot!" protested Michael, fake hurt.

I laughed. "Oh, come on, Mikey!" I said, and resumed walking toward his house. He fell in to step beside me. There were a couple of minutes of extremely awkward silence. But then I tripped over a pinecone that was lying on the sidewalk and we both had to laugh at my klutziness.

Journalist Overwhelmed by Anger, Embarrassment, and Love, Not Necessarily in That Order.

★   ★   ★

At Michael's, I laid out all of the research I had done to date on sleep and printing, as well as my list of questions for Mr. Dunleavy. Michael and I were all business after our little sidewalk chat, and I think it was comforting to us both to fall back into that routine and that way of talking to each other. That way we didn't have to deal with all that other awkward stuff.

"Okay, here's what I have so far on sleep . . . ," I began.

"Wait. Don't you think we should do the science project first?" asked Michael.

I cocked my head. "Well, we were assigned the article first," I reasoned.

"Yes, but the science project is for a grade. It's academic. I think it kind of beats the extracurricular."

"Hmm," I said. He had a point. "But it is optional. . . ."

"Yes, but we have *opted* to do it," pressed Michael.

I thought for a minute. "What's the worst thing that could happen if we don't hand in the article on time?" I asked.

"We let down Mr. Trigg, but he already loves us," said Michael with a shrug and a little grin. "And they run a file article in our place and our story runs the following week."

"Or sometime in the future when they need to fill a hole," I said snippily. "A file article!"

"Paste, I'm not sure what you have against file articles, but it can't be all breaking news all the time. Life just isn't like that."

"Mine is!" I said.

"That is a pretty stressful way to lead your life. Is that the kind of reporter you want to be? Like a war zone correspondent?"

I hesitated for a fraction of a second and then I nodded vigorously, but Michael spied the hesitation and pounced. "You seriously want to be living out of a backpack in the Middle East or Africa, fearing for your life, trying to file stories over crummy and unreliable Internet while you wonder if your sources are still alive?"

I just stared at him. "How do you know so much about that life?"

"I've read about it, seen movies, TV shows. I thought about it. But that is *not* the life for me. I'd rather challenge the bad guys here in the good old US of A." He grinned. "But I couldn't live with the day to day stress of a war zone. Anyway, I need my sleep and my creature comforts."

"Yeah, like your cinnamon buns!" I teased.

"Exactly."

I put my chin in my hand and thought about it for a minute. "I guess I just want to be at the forefront of where the action is. I like the urgency of a hot story."

"I get that. But it doesn't mean that every week has to be like that. It's so stressful and you'll kill yourself trying to make deadlines. It's like writing a column! Always trying to think up something clever or relevant on deadline. Something fresh. It would be horrible for me."

I almost blurted, "Tell me about it!" but I

caught myself in the nick of time and managed a noncommittal, "Yeah."

"Anyway, that's why I want to focus on the science project, okay?"

"Wow, that's a roundabout way of telling me, but okay, I guess, if you feel that strongly about it." I shrugged and handed him my list of questions for Mr. Dunleavy.

Meanwhile, I opened the link to the FlyPrint video from an e-mail I'd forwarded to Michael's computer and began to watch it.

Michael read my question list and half watched the video with me. He had lots to add to the question list (annoying because, as usual, he'd taken no notes last night). He wanted to know how much recycled paper FlyPrint used and where they got it and whether they recycled their own paper and damaged discards. He wanted to know whether the ink was unhealthy for the workers or for readers. He wanted to know about worker risk and injury.

"He'll never tell you that stuff about the workers!" I said. "And why would we want to include it in the science project?" I added, narrowing my eyes suspiciously.

Michael shrugged. "Just looking for an angle."

"It's not an article, though," I said.

"I know. But it might be. You said so last night."

Now it was my turn to shrug.

"A file article!" teased Michael, and I had to smile.

"Well, it's a project first, I guess, and we should focus on the science of it first. Here's the flow chart I did, showing the chain of events from harvesting the trees for paper through to recycling by the end user." I set it out in front of him.

"Pasty, this is really good!" said Michael with a low whistle as he looked over the page. "When did you find the time to do all this?"

I shrugged.

"You're a hard worker," he said, looking up at me. He gave me a warm smile.

"Thanks, I think."

"I still feel like I'm piggybacking on all your hard work."

"That's okay. I like working with you. And you

always come through in the end."

Michael burst out with a laugh. "I don't like the sound of that! Like you do all the front work and I come in at the eleventh hour?"

I raised my eyebrows and looked away for a second.

Michael looked at me until I looked back at him. "Is that what you think?"

"Sometimes. But this time I just took the initiative because it was interesting to me. No worries."

"All right, well, then why don't you let me do the call with Mr. Dunleavy? Then I will have started to approach your level of effort to date," he offered.

"Oh no. I don't mind calling Mr. Dunleavy," I said. "I told him I would. . . ."

"Sam!" said Michael. "You've got to stop being such a control freak. You can't do every single thing in life by yourself. Especially when you have a partner who wants to help you! I will call him! Now, what else can I do?" He scanned my notes while I thought of my mom and her comments about feathers and nests. I gulped.

Michael continued. "Get poster board, find images, type up overview. I'll do all that. Lay out flow chart: kind of already done by you." Here he stopped to fake glare at me; then he continued. "Do project title headline. Hey, do you think we'll be able to fit this all on one poster board or should we tape two together?" he asked.

"Oh, that's a good idea. Let's do two. Anyway, there *are* two of us. Maybe that way we could sketch it out and each work on half and finalize it at home. What do you think?"

"Totally," agreed Michael.

We got busily to work and Michael dialed Mr. Dunleavy and began chatting away. I stopped to listen to him and was really impressed. He handled himself like an adult on the phone and was very polite while still getting the answers he needed.

Breaking News: Watching Guys Work Makes Girls Swoon!

When he hung up, he looked at me sheepishly. "Well? Tell me the truth. How'd I do?" he asked.

"Great," I said with a grin.

There was a pause and then he said, "That's all? No more comments from the audience?"

"Nope. You did a great job."

"Huh. The control freak is softening," he teased.

I whacked him with a sheaf of paper and he laughed. "I've got miles to go before I sleep," I said, quoting the Robert Frost poem.

"Then let's get cracking!" he said.

Chapter 8

INVESTIGATIVE REPORTER TURNS GUINEA PIG FOR SAKE OF JOURNALISM!

★ ★ ★

So after all my research at Michael's house, I am now an expert on sleep. No joke. We did a lot of Internet searching, we called the National Sleep Foundation to clarify a few points, we called my pediatrician (Michael's idea, and a great one!) for some quotes, and we read some parenting books his mom had on the shelf. Here are some of the things I learned:

- ✔ Good sleep habits are called "sleep hygiene," and mine are terrible.
- ✔ I should never consume caffeine after noon (good-bye, afterschool diet cola!).
- ✔ The worst thing you can do is have a

digital clock shining in your face because its rays stimulate your brain (oops!).

✔ You should limit screen time (iPhone, computer, even TV) for at least an hour before bed (double oops!).

And here are some of the things I should be doing:

✔ exercising every day (no wonder Hailey sleeps so well!)

✔ going to bed and waking up at the same time every day (good-bye, lazy weekend mornings!)

✔ opening my window or turning down the heat so my room is cool

✔ taking a cool rather than hot shower shortly before bed (in the dim light, according to Mr. Trigg!)

✔ having a light snack an hour before bed

✔ wearing socks to sleep

✔ reading before bed

✔ having a fan on for white noise

✔ following a strict bedtime routine that lets my brain know it's getting toward sleep time

✔ not talking on the phone in bed; it needs to be a place only for relaxing and sleeping.

Okay, no problem, right? *Wrong!* It was a lot to remember. Do this; don't do that. It was sort of stress inducing in and of itself!

The bottom line, though, is that you need to make sure all of your bodily distractions are taken care of (you can't be hungry, too hot, or too cold; there can't be too much noise or too much light) and that you've tired yourself out enough (exercise; cool shower makes your body work harder to warm up and that is tiring), and you have to build in cues to make your body know it's bedtime (reading, white noise sound, etc.). It was almost too easy to be true.

Michael and I decided it would be cool for us both to do a three-day experiment and report our findings in the article. We decided we'd do our first night as we usually do, and then the next two nights we'd use good sleep hygiene and see if it paid off. I thought it could be really interesting and hey, the worst thing that could happen is I'd get a good night's sleep! (***Investigative Reporter Turns Guinea Pig for Sake of Journalism!***)

The timing was perfect because of Hailey sleeping over tonight. It wasn't like I could invite her and then just put on my socks and get in bed at nine thirty, right? I had to make it a little jazzy (bad sleep hygiene, here I come!). The plan was still for us to go downtown for pizza and then hit the mall for a little retail therapy. I called her as soon as I got home from Michael's and she said she'd be over in an hour.

"And I can't wait to show you my hair!" she trilled.

"Oh, phew. Good. Can't wait to see the improvement."

Before Hailey came over I had just enough time to organize all the materials and notes from my session at Michael's; then I showered and got ready for our outing.

★　　★　　★

I was watching TV when Hailey arrived. I heard the door open—Hailey never rings the bell—

and she called, "Anybody home?"

"Down here!" I replied from the den.

I heard Hailey skip down the flight of stairs and I turned around. "Hey! How did your hair turn out?" I called. She appeared in the doorway grinning and I gasped.

"Don't you like it?" asked Hailey, holding out an imaginary skirt and twirling.

I was speechless, for Hailey's hair had obviously been taken back to normal and then all of the tips had been redyed electric blue.

By the time I found my voice, Hailey's smile had faded. She stomped into the den and flopped on the couch. "You hate it," she cried, crossing her arms. "Now I hate it too!"

"No . . . I . . ."

"See?" she said.

"Wait. Hailey. I was just surprised. I mean, you hated the pink, and you had to get it out. Then Allie was helping, and I was expecting . . . well . . . not this!" I said. "But it's . . . kind of cute. I . . . I think I'll get used to it. It's better than the pink!" I added cheerily.

"Better than the pink. I have to remember that. It's the weakest compliment I've ever received. Huh . . ." Hailey sighed heavily. "I mean, I know it's silly. But it seemed like a good idea at the time. And Allie swore it was cool. She said all the high school girls are coloring their hair ends bright colors."

I rolled my eyes. "You know you have to take Allie with a grain of salt. Did she dye her own hair too?" I realized I hadn't seen her since Hailey was over this afternoon.

Hailey shook her head slowly, and I smacked my forehead. "Of course she didn't! What was I thinking?" I said with a laugh.

"What was *I* thinking?" Hailey wailed suddenly.

"Look, Allie has that effect on people. She can make anyone do anything. Don't worry about it. It's just, I guess it's because you have short hair, it's more noticeable. But hey, I like it better already. I mean, by later tonight I won't even be noticing it anymore. For real."

Hailey ruffled her fingers though her hair.

"Oh whatever, right? I can always rinse it out or cut my hair or something. It's kind of fun. At least for the weekend. That's what Allie said."

"Well, whatever *Allie* says . . . ," I said sarcastically.

Hailey chose to ignore that comment. "Okay, so when are we going out?" she asked, squinting at the cable box.

"I'm ready!" I said, jumping up. We needed a change of scenery.

"Me too!" she agreed.

Hailey and I went upstairs to ditch Hailey's bag and get my mom to drive us.

★ ★ ★

Can I just say that Slices pizza is really the best food on earth? I mean, if I could choose only one thing to eat for the rest of my life, it would be Slices pizza. It's thin and crispy on the bottom. There's not too much sauce or cheese, it's perfectly seasoned, a tiny bit salty, and washed down by an icy diet cola? Yum!

Hailey and I each had three slices and then walked over to the mall. We saw a few kids we knew in both places, but no one special (like you know who, of course!). Hailey usually has some crush going, but she's in a dry spell these days so we were just focused on ourselves, not chasing any guy around the mall. It was relaxing, actually. We played with smart phones and tablets in one store, tried on makeup in another, shot baskets at the sporting goods store, stopped for some ice cream, and actually had a really good time. It had been so long since I just chilled, it felt great.

Just as we were getting ready to call my mom to pick us up, we turned a corner and came face-to-face with whom else but Molly Grant. Her hair was still bright pink, even though she had a baseball cap crushed low over her face.

"Hailey! OMG, your hair looks amazing!" she gushed instantly. Her two friends nodded and smiled enthusiastically when Molly turned to them for confirmation.

Hailey blushed and ruffled her hair like she always does when she's embarrassed or nervous.

"Oh yeah, thanks." She shrugged. "Sam's

sister did it for me earlier."

"I love it! It's so cool!" said Molly. "So much better than the pink!"

That seemed to be the going compliment these days.

"Yeah, well . . . thanks . . . ," said Hailey, who seemed determined to keep walking and not stop to chat with these people.

But Molly wasn't going to let Hailey get away that easily.

"What are you guys up to here?" asked Molly.

"A little of this, a little of that," Hailey said. I could tell she was still annoyed around Molly, despite the teary bathroom scene earlier.

"Just getting ready to wrap it up," I added. I pulled out my phone and texted my mom for a ride. "What are *you* guys up to?" I asked, just to be polite.

"Well, we saw the new Anne Hathaway movie. It was sooo awesome! Then we had dinner in the food court. And now we're kind of just walking around. Hailey, what's *your* favorite store?" asked Molly.

Hailey just shrugged and smiled. I knew there was no way she was giving Molly any more information.

My phone buzzed with an incoming message and I looked down. It was from my mom and it said, *Find Allie. She's there too. Then txt me. Will pick u up together.*

I laughed. "Hey, Allie's here somewhere," I said.

"She is?" Hailey perked right up.

"Oh, that's your sister, right? Who's in high school?" asked Molly.

"Uh, yeah."

"Where is she?" asked Hailey eagerly. "Want me to text her?"

Annoying that Hailey has Allie's number but whatever. "Sure." I shrugged.

Hailey eagerly began punching into her phone.

Seconds later, her phone buzzed back. "Oh, they're at the tea place," said Hailey. "Let's go. Bye!" she said to Molly and her friends.

"See you guys!" I said.

"Um . . . ," Molly began. "Hey! I mean, is there any way I could come with you guys and find out about getting the pink out?"

I looked at Hailey. She was not psyched but couldn't figure out how to say no politely. I wished I could help her, but we were kind of on the spot. We both hesitated for a second and then Molly said, "Thanks," and started walking along with us. Her friends hung back at a polite distance. After all, it's not like seventh and eighth graders ever really hang out, you know? At least *they* understood the rules.

Hailey basically ignored Molly on the walk over to the tea store, so I had to do all the answering (because Molly did all the questioning). By the time we reached the tea shop, Molly knew where Hailey gets her hair cut, who Hailey thinks has the best shoe selection in the mall, what kind of moisturizer Hailey uses, and Hailey's favorite brand of jeans. I felt thoroughly interrogated. I actually considered asking her if she'd ever thought of joining the *Cherry Valley Voice* as a reporter, but I wasn't sure I could stand to be around her that much. She definitely had a future in the CIA if she wanted it.

Allie was sitting at a table inside with her friends, and she rolled her eyes when we arrived, which didn't stop Hailey from waving enthusiastically at her from outside the plate-glass window of the shop.

"Stop. She won't like that. And then we'll suffer," I said to Hailey, pulling her hand down.

Hailey shrugged. "She waved back."

Allie continued sitting inside and chatting with her friends as if we were of utterly no consequence to her. I tried to catch her eye to indicate that we were ready to leave, but she wouldn't look my way. I sighed heavily in frustration. Going in to get her was not an option. Allie would come when Allie was good and ready. Until then we'd just have to wait.

"So is she coming?" asked Molly hopefully.

"Eventually," I said with an eye roll.

"Maybe you should just write in to Dear Know-It-All about fixing that hair," suggested one of Molly's friends, giggling. My ears perked up at the name of my column.

"That would take too long!" replied Molly. "It doesn't come out until next week."

"Plus the answers haven't been so great lately," said Molly's other friend.

I restrained myself from attacking her. *Journalist Blows Cover in Mall Brawl.* Can you just imagine?

"Well, they've been shorter, but they're just as good as ever," said Molly.

Did I ever say Molly was annoying? I take it back. I wanted to thank her but couldn't do that either.

"I guess," said her friend.

Molly continued. "It's just . . . it seems like lately it's like Know-It-All has been in a rush, you know?"

The other girls agreed. Inwardly, I cringed, knowing it was true. *Feathers, nest, you know the rest.*

Now Hailey joined in. "I agree. I look forward to reading it every week. I mean, I feel like Know-It-All is my friend! Sometimes it's like she reads my mind. Spooky," said Hailey with a little shudder.

She is *your friend, you dope!* I wanted to yell, but obviously I couldn't. I distracted myself by staring daggers at Allie, hoping she'd turn and look out here so I could signal her to go.

Molly and her friends got into a side discussion of where they wanted to go next, and Hailey slid down the outside window of the shop to sit on the floor. I couldn't bring myself to join her. It would mean we had totally surrendered to Allie's schedule.

"Hey, um, excuse me, but would it be all right to go in there and just ask your sister what she did to get the pink out earlier?" asked Molly. "'Cause we have to go."

"Suit yourself," I said with a shrug.

"Thanks," said Molly, and I watched as she entered the shop, marched right over to Allie, and began chatting her up. Allie looked a little surprised by the interruption at first, but when Molly lifted off her hat, Allie and her friends all began chattering at once and gesturing, and Molly was laughing, and then so were they. *What-ever*, I thought, turning away.

"What are you making for the bake sale?" asked Hailey, picking at her fingernails. "My mom says I can make carrot cupcakes," she added with a frown of distaste.

I stared at her blankly. "What bake sale?"

Hailey looked up quickly. "Seriously?"

"Um . . . ," I said.

Hailey slid back up the wall until she was facing me. "You're joking, right?"

"No . . . I . . . ," I stammered. Was there a bake sale I was supposed to know about?

Sighing in exasperation, Hailey said, *"Hell-o?* The bake sale to raise money for the new computers in the library? This Thursday? I signed you up to bring three things. We discussed this!"

"We did?" I said.

Hailey laughed. "You're a pretty good joker," she said. "You actually fooled me for a minute."

"I'm not joking," I said, because I wasn't. "And I can't do it. I have an article due and a huge science project, not to mention my regular work." *And my column*, I added silently.

Hailey narrowed her eyes and looked at me. "I was counting on you. Rice Krispies treats, cupcakes, and those insane chocolate chip cookies your mom makes. This is one of my first duties as vice president of the student council. It was my idea, and it has to be a success!" She was starting to get worked up.

"Um . . ." Mentally I tried to think of all the ways my mom had made me practice saying no. But the thing was, a tiny bell was ringing in the back of my mind that I had, actually, agreed to this a while back. "Well . . ."

Hailey glared at me.

"Okay?" I said halfheartedly. Another feather from my nest.

"Thanks," said Hailey grimly.

I glanced inside. Molly and Allie and their friends were all still yukking it up. Suddenly I was exhausted and I wished that tonight was a good sleep hygiene night for the experiment instead of a bad one. I texted my mom.

Ready. Thx., it said.

Then I rapped on the window with my knuckles and waved Allie out. She looked at me in surprise, as if how dare I tell her when to leave, but she did begin (very slooowly) putting on her coat and picking up her things.

Out came Molly, though, who said, "OMG! Your sister is so awesome! She invited me over tomorrow to help with my hair! Isn't that sooo unbelievably nice?"

"Yes. It is unbelievable," I said.

"Wow, you Martone girls are the best. Almost as cool as Hailey Jones!" she joked.

Easy there, seventh grader, I wanted to say, but I didn't.

"Thanks," I said instead. Then I nudged Hailey.

"What? Oh. Thanks. Bye," she said, clearly disinterested.

Molly left and finally, finally Allie rolled out, laughing. "I should open a beauty salon!" she said.

Hailey perked right up on her arrival. "Totally!

You'd be great at it!" she said supportively.

I rolled my eyes and said, "Let's go. Mom's going to be downstairs any second."

On the car ride home, Allie and Hailey chattered about Allie opening a hair salon and I tuned them out, wondering how I'd ever get everything done this week.

Chapter 9

DROWNING GIRL SOBS AS LIFEBOAT TURNS OUT TO BE ILLUSION

★ ★ ★

Well, my bad sleep hygiene went well. Hailey and I stayed up way past midnight and slept until ten a.m. on Saturday. We were on Buddybook till all hours, with my computer on my bed, drinking more Diet Coke, and we basically broke all the good sleep hygiene rules we could. Tonight I was sure I'd pay.

However, in the interest of following all the good sleep rules, I went to Hailey's soccer practice with her and I ran/walked laps around the track while she played. (Okay, I mostly walked, but still.) It was kind of boring, but I knew it was all for the sake of my article so I went along with it.

We went back to my house after and Molly

was there with Allie. They each had a friend with them. It was kind of like a dream—Molly Grant in my house with my sister? Weird. But they were having a grand old time and Hailey had to go. I wasn't about to hang around with that strange group, so I decided to have a quick PB and J, then pack up and head to the library, where I could get some work done.

Once there, I found a table in a quiet area and went to fill my water bottle, when whom should I spot but a familiar hunky shape huddled over a desk.

"Psst! Mikey!" I whispered.

He jolted up and looked at me in surprise.

"Were you asleep?" I asked quietly, stifling a laugh.

"Me? What? No." He rubbed his eyes and blinked a few times. "Maybe."

I wagged my finger at him. "Remember, no naps today! It's a good sleep hygiene day."

Michael grinned and his dimples deepened. My heart soared. "How did last night go for you?" he asked.

"It was awful. I broke every single rule, I think."

"Good." He nodded. "Me too."

"How's the project going?" I asked.

Michael shook his head. "Okay. Not great. I got bogged down in researching the article instead. It was kind of more fun," he admitted.

"See? I told you. You're the one who wanted to prioritize the science thing."

"Yeah, well, I still think we should. Have you done anything else on it?"

"A little, but that's why I'm here."

Michael nodded. "Well, we probably shouldn't sit together. We'll never get anything done."

It was kind of a backhanded compliment, but it still stung a little. "Right," I agreed, trying to seem businesslike. He *was* right, after all.

"So I'll see you around. Where are you sitting?" he asked. I pointed out my table.

"I'll stop by before I go. Okay, Pasty?"

I nodded and waved and set off for my desk.

It was kind of distracting and a bummer knowing Michael, cutie-pie crush of my life, was in the same building as me and I couldn't hang with him. Especially because the majority of what I was working on (article and project) were things I was doing with him! I tried to focus on getting work done. If I didn't, this week would be a nightmare. That fear and the lack of other distractions (besides ML!) allowed me to really concentrate.

I drafted a really good sidebar with a timeline of printing technology and developments for the science poster. I was psyched about that. I planned out my side of the flow chart and did a little rough paragraph for each stage. I'd edit it later and then print out the final versions, cut them out, and paste them on the poster board in order. I was basically finished with the poster. Yay!

Tapping my teeth with a pen, I considered drafting Michael's mini paragraphs, too, just as a gift. I was on such a roll, I could have easily whipped them off. But I knew he'd get mad at me, and that's the last thing I wanted. A tiny part of me regretted—just for a flash instant—partnering on this project. I could have finished it this weekend on my own, after all. I mean, I'm glad to have one more reason to talk to Michael, but I'm starting to think maybe it's better to keep love and academics separate.

Next I mapped out an outline for our sleep article, laying out which paragraphs would be about what and what the two sidebars would cover. I was really cooking!

I decided I had time for one more thing, so I took out my trusty journalist's notebook and began brainstorming a few things I could say in my DKIA column. (Like, 'Make use of the weekends to get stuff done. Long blocks of time can reduce workload.' Or 'Practice saying No or Maybe to your friends so you don't agree to everything when they put you on the spot.'). Suddenly I felt a tap on my shoulder and I jumped about three feet in the air.

Michael chuckled. "Sorry, Paste."

I put my hand to my chest to slow my rapidly beating heart. "Don't do that to people. A little warning, please?"

Michael shrugged, his light blue eyes still twinkling. "It's a library. You're supposed to be quiet."

"Hmmm," I grumbled. "Are you done?"

Michael looked away. "No, but I have to go."

"Why?"

"Basketball tryouts."

"Oh. Did you get a lot done?"

"Sort of. Mostly homework for Monday." He shrugged.

"Okay. So . . ."

Michael looked back at me. "I'm going to work on the science project tonight. And the article. As soon as I get home. I'm all fired up. I promise."

I hoped so. We were getting down to the wire a little. I didn't want to say anything mean, but . . . Instead, I decided to keep it light. "Just remember, early to bed and early to rise!"

Michael saluted me and smiled in relief I'd let him off so easy. "Got it! See ya later, Pasty. Wish me luck!"

"Good luck!" I whispered as he walked away. "Wish me luck, too!" I added even more quietly. ***Drowning Girl Sobs as Lifeboat Turns Out to Be Illusion.***

★   ★   ★

At eight thirty that night I went downstairs in my house to eat a few crackers and then say good night to my mother. I had taken a cool shower and

I was in my pj's and socks. I hadn't looked at my computer or the TV for more than an hour.

"Samantha! What a surprise! Are you feeling well?" She put her cool palm on my forehead.

I laughed. "Yes. It's part of my sleep project. I'm using good sleep hygiene tonight."

"Well, that is just the best news I've heard all week!" she cheered. Giving me a hug she continued. "Is everything going okay?"

I nodded a little, which was difficult because my head was wedged under her chin. She held me away and looked into my eyes.

"I'm good," I said. And it was pretty true.

"School okay? Friends okay? Newspaper okay?"

"Yup."

"How's the prioritizing going?"

"Good," I said, thinking of Michael's not working on our project.

"How's the saying no to friends going?"

"Great," I said, thinking of Hailey's upcoming bake sale.

My mom looked at me carefully. I crossed my

toes inside my socks. "Okay," she said finally. "Just remember to look out for yourself, all right, sweetheart?"

I nodded. "'Night, Mom!"

"Good night, my love."

Back upstairs, I made sure my window was open a crack to let in the cool air. I set up the fan I usually use in the summer. Its whirring sound would make me feel like I was sleeping in a car or on a train or something, but that might be okay. (I've obviously proved that sleeping in cars is easy for me.) I dimmed my lights, tightly closed my shades and curtains, set my alarm for seven a.m., and flipped the clock facedown. Then I went to brush my teeth in the darkened bathroom.

Of course, while I was in there, Allie came barreling in, flipping on the light. She jumped when she saw me. I squinted at her in the mirror.

"Sam! What are you doing in here in the dark? With the light out, I didn't think anyone was in here!"

"Can you turn it off, please?" I said through my toothpaste.

"Why?" asked Allie, but she did. She stood in the doorway while I spit and rinsed.

"Sleep project," I said, blotting my mouth on a towel. "Now get out, please. I need some privacy for a minute and then it's all yours."

Annoyingly, she waited for me. Outside, I clicked the hall light off and explained everything to her in the dim light. She obviously found my sleep hygiene boring because she immediately changed the subject.

"Your friend Molly is so cute. Or, I should say, Hailey's friend."

"She's neither of our friends. She's not even in our grade."

"Really?" said Allie, turning on the light to look at me. "Well, she talks about you all like you're friends."

I sighed and snapped the light off. "I'm sure. Please tell me you didn't give her Hailey's exact hair?"

"Why?" asked Allie, flicking the light switch back on. She obviously had. "That's what she wanted."

"Aargh!" I slapped my forehead; then I smacked off the light. "I meant to tell you, but Hailey was here and then Molly herself so I couldn't. Molly drives Hailey *crazy* copying her. Now Hailey will be back to have the blue taken out—mark my words—then Molly will be back for the same. You're going to have to start charging. Good night." I couldn't take any more of this frustrating conversation. I'd be too riled up to fall asleep.

Allie turned the light back on and stood there with her arms folded. I took one last look and could see an idea brewing on her face and I wanted no part in it. I closed my eyes against the hall light and speed-walked to my room.

Inside, I arranged my notebook next to my bedside table in case I needed to jot anything down. Then I climbed into my bed with a kind of mild book (no spy thrillers tonight!), and started to read. I read for about half an hour, and then guess what? I began to feel really drowsy! So I turned off my light and went to sleep! Just like that!

And do you know what was the best part? I

slept all night until my alarm woke me up at seven a.m. the next day!

The only bummer is there's not that much to do at seven a.m. on a Sunday. Everyone else is asleep and nothing's open. There's nowhere to go. I wanted to text Michael because, according to our plan, he should have been up by now, but in case he wasn't, I didn't want his phone to wake him. Instead I watched some TV and tried to stay awake. Eventually Hailey called and we made a plan to exercise together and the day got rolling. But it was a long one (especially since I couldn't have caffeine!).

It wasn't until I'd exercised with Hailey, eaten lunch, and was printing out the final versions of my mini paragraphs for my flowchart that the phone rang and it was for me.

"It's lover boy!" whispered Allie, barely covering the phone with her hand.

I tried to punch her, but she quickly ducked out of my way.

Girl Seethes with Plot for Revenge as Perpetrator Escapes!

"Hello?" I made myself sound really neutral and not excited at all.

"Hey, Sam," said Michael. His voice was kind of squeaky, without its usual relaxed huskiness.

"What's wrong?" I asked; then immediately I wanted to kick myself. I bit my lip and closed my eyes. Why did I have to be so awkward around Michael sometimes?

He cleared his throat. "Um. Well. Since you asked . . . I . . . ahem. Sam."

"Michael, what is it?"

Michael spoke all in a rush. "Sam, I can't do the science project with you. I'm so sorry. I feel terrible."

"What?" I was shocked. "Why?"

"Well, I just . . . I shouldn't have said yes from the start. I'm going to have to take my low grade and maybe make it up another time, another way. I wanted to help you out and, I, um, I thought it would be fun to work on it with you since . . . well, we work well together or whatever. But I shouldn't have said yes. I'm just so buried. And my mom . . . well. She got mad at me for taking on too much stuff and doing none of it well. I guess I've just been spreading myself too thin."

I was silent for a minute. I was so stunned that he was having the exact same issues as me that I didn't know what to say.

"Sam? Are you there? I understand if you never want to talk to me . . ."

"Michael, stop! Please!" I laughed. "I totally understand. This is me you're talking to, remember?"

"Wait, what?" Michael sounded confused. "You're not furious? Because you have every right to be. I mean, I've totally dragged you down."

"I am going through all the same stuff as you! My mom is making me start saying no to stuff too! It's such a coincidence!"

"Oh!" Michael laughed a relieved laugh. "Really?"

"Yes! Please don't worry about it. I can pull it off all by myself. I can just use the stuff you disallowed me to use. . . ."

"Well, I can give you my Dunleavy transcript. . . ."

"No. I'll call him myself. It's better that way.

Thanks, though. And also, I don't mind if you still want to do the same project, but just by yourself and on your own timetable. I mean, you've already done at least half of the work. It would be kind of a waste."

"Thanks, Paste. I might."

"Sure."

We were quiet for a split second, and then we both spoke at the same time.

"Hey, so . . ."

"Well, what . . ."

We laughed.

"The article?" I said.

"Yeah, about the article. I think we're writing a file piece, Paste. I'm sorry. I know how you hate that, but there's just no way I can pull it off for this Thursday. Is that okay?"

I wasn't surprised. "It's fine. I totally get it. I'll let Mr. Trigg know when we hang up so he can start looking through his files to fill that spot."

"Thanks." Michael let out a huge sigh. "I was dreading this phone call, but now I feel much better."

"Yeah. It's hard to prioritize sometimes."

"Yeah. Especially 'cause I always want to do stuff with you—" Michael stopped abruptly. "I mean . . ."

"Right," I said, covering for him. "We work well together."

"Yes. That's what I meant."

We both laughed a little awkwardly.

"Thanks for letting me know, Mikey. Good luck."

"Thank you, Pasty. Thanks a lot. I mean it."

"Bye."

I hung up the phone and sat there for a minute. Who'd have thought that Mr. Together, Mr. Photographic Memory, Mr. All-Around Athlete and Scholar would be having the same problems I was having? I wrapped my arms around myself in happiness, though, thinking of how he said he always wanted to do stuff with me. Even if he meant just as a friend, it was a nice confirmation.

Thinking about how he said it might keep me up all night, though!

Chapter 10

WOODWARD BETRAYS BERNSTEIN!

★ ★ ★

Shortly after the phone call from Michael, I fired off an e-mail to Mr. Trigg, asking if our sleep article could go to file and be replaced by something from the file. Then I e-mailed Mr. Dunleavy to see if we could set a call for four o'clock tomorrow afternoon. I didn't expect to hear back from either of them since it was a Sunday, but I was pleasantly surprised when I heard back from both within the hour.

Mr. Dunleavy readily agreed to the call, which was great. I just had a few remaining questions, a couple about recycling and the environment, two about their clients, and one about safety. Since Michael was no longer on the project, I had the freedom to ditch the labor angle. He could pick it back up when and if he decided to do his own project or if we did it as an article at a later date.

Mr. Trigg asked me to call him at home, so I did. As usual, he picked up right away.

"Ms. Martone, what a pleasant surprise! How is your weekend going?"

We chatted for a minute, and then he asked what was going on with the article.

I explained about the time crunch, but I also told him about our sleep experiment and the research we'd done to date.

"Hmm," said Mr. Trigg. I could picture him folding his arms and tapping his chin with his index finger, as he always does when he's thinking.

"What do you think about postponing it or making it a file article?" I asked.

"I certainly think it would be fine, but it sounds like you've done almost all the research and you just need to write it up?"

"Basically . . . ," I admitted.

"Is it you or Michael who doesn't have the time to work on it? Or is it both of you?"

Uh-oh. I didn't want to sell Michael out (*Woodward Betrays Bernstein!*) and honestly,

I still had quite a bit to do myself over the next three or four days: finishing my poster, writing the DKIA, baking for Hailey.

"Um . . ."

Mr. Trigg sensed my hesitation. "The only reason I ask is that I think the sleep article will dovetail so nicely with your Know-It-All this week. Certainly you'd have to be careful that they don't intertwine or refer to each other in any way or you'd be giving away your identity. But if you could possibly pull it off—even a condensed version of what you were hoping to do—I think it would be a nice opportunity for you to have your own byline and to flesh out what you'll touch on in your column."

"Oh," I said. "Well, can I think about it for a little while? I'd want to check with Michael too."

"Absolutely. Just decide maybe by tomorrow, alrighty?"

"Okay. Thanks, Mr. Trigg."

After we hung up, I sat at my desk and stared out the window at a little bird hopping around on a branch. It would be so easy to be a bird, I thought. All you have to do is build a nest (with lots of feathers) and find worms. Well, and maybe fly south for the winter. Oh and then get back up here for spring. And make sure your baby birds live. Yeah. Maybe it wouldn't be so easy to be a bird after all.

Chastened, I decided to make a list of everything I had to do. Then I'd go talk to my mom about everything.

★ ★ ★

Twenty minutes later, my mom had my list in front of her and she was twirling her hair, thinking.

"Well, I could do some of the baking for you. I don't mind. I have the time that night, and I'm happy to help Hailey out. I'm so proud of her job on student council," said my mom. "Maybe Allie would help too."

I scoffed. "Right."

"Samantha, please. Allie has been very nice to you lately, and she is also a big fan of Hailey's."

"And Molly's," I added.

"Oh yes, that lovely girl who was here the other day. Right! Is she working on the bake sale, too?"

"No, that's not what I meant, but . . ." Suddenly I had a eureka moment. "Hey! Hey, Mom! You are a genius!" I jumped up and gave her a hug. "Can I use the phone for a minute? I have to call Hailey!"

My mom had a confused look on her face, but she handed me the phone and I speed-dialed Hailey.

Luckily, she answered.

"Hails. Genius idea by my mom. Have Molly do a bunch of baking for you for the bake sale this week!"

"Hello, to you too, Samantha," said Hailey formally.

"Seriously, what do you think?"

Hailey was quiet for a second. "But if I ask her for a favor, then do I owe her one?"

"You dope, she owes you one! You got Allie to do her hair, remember? Which, by the way, is apparently identical to yours again but never mind," I said in a really fast rush. "Anyway, she worships you so much, I'm sure she'd do it even if she didn't owe you a favor."

"Hmm. You do have a point. Okay. I am

ignoring something you just said about her hair. Ignoring! Ignoring! So will you ask her about the baking or me?"

"You. It will mean more coming from you. She'll never be able to say no."

"Okay, I guess. Come with me though so you can lay on thickly how much it will mean to me, all right?"

We agreed to meet the next morning and track down Molly, and then we hung up.

"Genius, Mom. Thanks!" I said. I sat back down.

My mom looked pleased with herself. "I didn't realize I was suggesting anything, but I'm happy it worked out."

"Right. Now I don't feel as pressured to make three things. I think we could make one big double batch of your cookies and that's plenty, okay?"

"Sure. I can do that easily."

"Thanks. Now for the other stuff." I explained everything to my mom about the science project, the article, the column, and the other general homework and scheduling issues I had this week, plus my sleep issues (which seemed to be on the mend). She listened patiently. After I was finished, she thought for a minute. Then she said, "Okay. I have some advice. Not that you need to take it."

"Okay," I said.

"You can knock off the science today easily, right?"

I nodded.

"You can whip up the column tomorrow night, right?"

Again, I agreed.

"And I think you could probably pull off the article by Thursday too. It's just the Michael aspect that is tricky."

"Yes."

"What if you did that thing with the byline where you are the lead writer and then you put in 'Additional reporting by Michael Lawrence'?"

I cocked my head. "Huh."

"Do they ever do that at the *Cherry Valley Voice*?"

I shrugged. "I don't know, but I'm sure we could. I just wonder if Michael would be mad if

I went ahead without him."

My mom spoke gently. "Sam, I don't want to push you. You're on the verge of being overloaded again, and only you can decide how much you can really handle while still getting to bed at a good hour. But I also think you have to see that Michael is learning how to put himself first sometimes, just like you. I think it would be okay to finish the article, give him the credit he deserves, and submit it. Put yourself first this time."

I laughed a little. "It's funny because we just practiced saying no to more work and more stuff, and now I have to work on saying yes, too."

"I know. Life is funny that way. Things change quickly. You need to be flexible and always be reprioritizing."

I nodded. "I'm going to use that in my column."

"What column?" said Allie, bounding into the room.

Older Sister Training for CIA; Could Beat Any Spy.

I blanched and, astoundingly, my mom covered

for me. "Mr. Trigg is devoting a whole column of the front page to your sister's article this week. It might become a regular feature on health."

My eyes widened at my mother's fib, and when Allie looked at me for verification, I caught my mom winking at me over Allie's shoulder. I had to stifle my smile.

"Is that true?" asked Allie.

I shrugged casually. "We've tossed it around. He'd like me to write a regular column one day maybe."

Allie considered this. "Too bad you didn't get that Dear Know-It-All job, then."

I nodded. "Yeah," I said. "Too bad."

My mom stepped in again, luckily. "Anyway, dear, why don't you go upstairs and think it all over, okay?"

I stood up. "Thanks, Mom."

"Anytime," she said with a grin and another wink. "Anytime."

I trudged back upstairs to my room, dreading what I knew I must do. I held the portable phone in my hand and sat down heavily at my desk. (I was going to sit on my bed to make the call, but that would have been bad sleep hygiene!) I took a deep breath and dialed the number I know by heart.

"Is Michael there, please? It's Samantha Martone," I said when his dad answered.

Michael picked up a second later. "Sam?"

"Hey."

"What's up?"

I sighed and then I explained about the call with Mr. Trigg. Halfway through my explanation, Michael interrupted. "Sam, Sam, please. You don't need to explain. Honestly, you'd be doing me a favor if you took it over. And you don't need to give me a reporting credit. Honestly, I did nothing but look at some parenting books with you. It was your idea from the beginning anyway."

"No. I'd give you credit. You've worked on it a bunch with me, and I wouldn't feel right otherwise."

"Sam, seriously. Go ahead and do it and please do not give it another thought. I could really use the break, and I'm happy to have you soldier on.

Okay? I'm actually grateful. For real. I'll even bake you cinnamon buns to prove it. Just not for a very long time," he said, laughing.

I laughed too. Now it was my turn to feel relieved. "Thanks. I'll look forward to that when I'm old and gray and in the home, Drooly. Listen, seriously though. I really appreciate it."

"It's funny, me calling you to beg off from the work and then you calling me to ask for more. Maybe you should do an article on time management next!" suggested Michael.

I winced; that was so close to my Know-It-All for this week. "Oh no. Not me. I don't know anything about that!" I protested.

"Don't sell yourself short, Pasty. You're a pro at it. And hey, good luck. Thanks for thinking of me in all this."

"Thanks, Mikey. Talk to you later."

I hung up the phone and looked out the window again. The bird was gone from its branch. Probably battling cold winds and mean, bigger birds, struggling its way south. Or maybe . . . maybe it had first flown to visit its own mama bird, who was feeding it a nice meal and letting it stay in her well-feathered nest until it felt strong enough to make the big flight. That idea made me smile, and I set to work finishing the other half of the science poster.

Chapter 11

JOURNALIST HAS THE LAST WORD. REJOICES IN VICTORY!

★ ★ ★

I woke up early the next morning, fully refreshed by a great night's sleep. The good sleep hygiene thing was no joke, and I was so excited to work it into my article for the paper. I really enjoyed being my own test subject. It could be a really cool form of journalism that I'd like to pursue—the kind where you put yourself in the center of an experiment (learning a new skill, testing a new product or health regime, trying to quit saying "like") and then write about it. It would certainly beat reporting from the front lines of a war, the way Michael described it.

Hailey and I attacked Molly with our enthusiasm right before the first bell rang, and by recess we had her and three of her buddies committed to bringing seven more things for the bake sale!

Unfortunately, I didn't get to see Michael all day, even though I looked for him everywhere. I even wondered if he might have been sick, but Hailey said she saw him in the library working when she met with her tutor during lunch, so I knew he was just muscling through and getting stuff done. I was proud of him and very, very sympathetic.

After school, I had my call with Mr. Dunleavy, who gave me a few more good tidbits to finalize the poster. Then I set to work typing up the remainder of my mini paragraphs for that and taping them and my final sidebar all down to the double poster boards. I was sure to get an A plus on it!

Tuesday morning, I brought the poster into school, hoping I'd see Michael so I could show it to him. I didn't want to call and make a plan to meet him—I wanted it to just happen. But it didn't. Maybe that was for the better, anyway. At lunch I turned the poster in to Dr. Shenberg, and the expression on his face told me he was pleased. He said Michael had already talked to him about bowing out of the project and that they'd work something out another time. I was relieved, but I was still a little sad about how it all worked out for us with this project. Michael had been pretty into it, especially when we went on the field trip. (I still cringe every time I think of how I fell asleep.)

That afternoon, I worked a little bit on my sleep article and I finished my column. I was pretty psyched about it. Here is what I said:

Dear Stressin',

I know how you feel. Eighth grade is no joke, and there's so much to fit in—fun stuff and work. But stressing only makes things worse. My advice is to learn to put yourself first, in a nice way. Make sure you prioritize (schoolwork does come first at our age, unfortunately) and then you should save time to get the things done that matter for your health and well-being (see my list below). Extra things come last. Most important, you need to be flexible and always be reprioritizing.

Also, you'd be surprised how understanding and flexible your friends and teachers can be if you take the time to talk to them about your workload or schedule before things get out of control. Don't be shy. Ask for help and don't be afraid to say no to friends' plans and requests for your time. They will still like you. And don't forget that your parents and even your siblings can be your biggest helpers if only you ask.

If you start to feel stressed, follow this checklist:

SLEEP: Did you get enough last night?

EXERCISE: Did you get some today?

SUNLIGHT: Did you spend time in the sun today?

NUTRITION: Make sure you are eating properly (not too much junk!).

WORK: Have you studied or done something productive today?

FRIENDS: Did you have a little fun or at least have some contact with your buds?

RELAXATION: Did you do something today that made you totally slow down and zone out?

LAUGHTER: Try to laugh a little every day even if it's only watching giggling baby videos on YouTube.

All of these things contribute to your physical well-being, and you wouldn't believe how important that is to your mental well-being. You can't be happy or feel peaceful if you're not eating well or sleeping well. Stress kills, so do everything you can to fight it off, and always remember, we are still kids. Nothing is life or death. If you start to feel it is, tell a trusted grown-up as soon as possible.

Good luck, and try to have some fun today!

Best wishes,

Know-It-All

Before I e-mailed it to Mr. Trigg, I showed my reply to my mom and she loved it, which made me feel really good. Of course, a lot of it was her advice, so maybe she was just happy I'd been paying attention!

It wasn't until Wednesday night that I began to really feel crunched. I had a math test on Thursday, plus the final draft of the sleep article. My mom was baking for Hailey's bake sale, but I didn't want to totally ditch her so I'd offered to do the dishes after. My mom said, "We'll see," but it was still my goal. I studied for my test and did a bunch of sample problems to test myself and then got a few other scraps of homework out of the way. Finally, it was time to tackle my final draft of "Sleep."

You won't believe it, but the sleep article kept me up all night!

First of all, I couldn't find a sheet of notes I'd taken at Michael's. I had to call him at nine o'clock, which is kind of late, and ask him if he could either scan the notes on his printer and e-mail them to me, or if he could read them over the phone. I felt guilty asking for his help again on something that was officially my project, and I hated to take time away from his work.

"What was it you said about not being a Last-Minute Lucy the other day?" he teased.

I gulped. "Um. Sorry about that. I guess we all have our moments."

"Just keeping you honest, Martone." He chuckled. He sounded like his old self.

"I haven't seen you this week," I said. I hoped it didn't sound clingy, so I quickly added, "I'm sure you've been super busy, and I'm glad you're getting your work done."

"Yeah. Thanks. I've been trying to get stuff done during the day, like at lunchtime, in the library. Also, I made the final cuts for the basketball team. I've been there every day after school. Actually . . . I . . . I don't want to brag, but I'm the captain this year, so that's kind of time-consuming."

"Michael! Congratulations! I can't believe that's not the first thing you told me! You jerk!"

He laughed. "Seriously? Like, 'Hi, Pasty. They made me captain of varsity basketball this year?'"

"Yes, just like that! That's what friends are for—to celebrate the good times with you!"

"Oh, I thought friends were for scanning things when you've left them till the last minute!" he teased.

"That too!" I said, laughing. "Thanks. And that's great news. I'm happy for you."

"Me too. I just hope I can juggle it all because . . . I just want to make sure we still have time together. I mean, you know . . . like, writing together and stuff," he finished awkwardly.

I couldn't hold back the grin that spread across my face. I was sure he could hear it in my voice, but I didn't mind. "Yeah. Me too. Well, thanks for your help with the article. I'll cc you when I send it to Trigger later."

"Hopefully not much later!" he said.

"Thanks."

I was still grinning when we hung up, and shortly thereafter came his e-mail with the sleep notes scanned into it. It said, "Good luck, Pasty!" and he signed it, "Xo, Michael"!!!! I couldn't believe it! Impulsively, I typed back, "Thanks! Xo, S" and hit send before I could chicken out. I pictured him getting it and smiling too.

But after that, my night took a turn for the worse. I was having a hard time getting a thesis going for the article, and I learned how much I'd come to rely on bouncing things off Michael when we were writing together. I tried a couple of lead sentences and noodled around with pulling out a different part for the sidebar, but I kept getting stuck. As the minutes ticked by, I found myself compulsively checking the red digital numbers and thinking about my old friend Diet Coke.

When my mom came in to check on me at ten thirty, she was dismayed. "Samantha, you should have been asleep by now. What about the new sleep regime?"

I shook my head sadly. "Ironic, isn't it? Up all night working on the sleep article."

"Oh, Sammy. I feel terrible, like I pushed you into doing it. I'm so sorry. You were trying to give yourself some breathing room in your schedule, and I was the one who encouraged you to just finish it." She went to sit on my bed, then remembered my sleep rules and stood back up.

I laughed. "It's okay. You can sit on the bed. I just can't!"

She sat down. "Is it too late to back out now?"

I nodded. "But you know what? It's okay. I know the tricks now to getting back into a good sleep routine. I know what it takes. And I don't feel alone, you know? I feel like you're involved, Michael cares, Mr. Trigg is in this with me. It's a good feeling. Sometimes when you feel like you're swamped and all alone, that's what makes it worse."

She bit her lip and looked at me sympathetically. "I'll stay up until you finish it."

"Mom, that's crazy! Why waste a good night's sleep of your own on this?"

"So you know you're not in it alone. I'm going to get my book, and then I'll come hang out with you. Be right back." In a flash, she was gone.

A few minutes later there was a tap on my door, and my mom reappeared with a small tray. The tray had two freshly baked gooey chocolate chip cookies and a glass of milk on it. She set it down on my desk and then settled back against my bed pillows to read. I ate the cookies and, after a minute, felt reenergized. I tried a new thesis for the article, one that would mean cutting out a whole section and leaving the article quite a bit shorter, but it was much better. I had gotten a little bogged down with the facts and they were holding me back. Now things were flowing. Within the hour, I was finished and spell-checking the article.

My mom was starting to yawn about every other minute, so I think my timing was good. At eleven thirty I sent it to Mr. Trigg and Michael (no "xo" this time!), and when I turned to tell my mom, she was asleep.

"Mom?" I whispered. Her eyes snapped open.

"Just resting!" she said, fake perky.

"I'm done," I said.

"Good for you!" She sat up and swung her feet to the floor. "By the way, meat is done; people are finished," she scolded.

I smiled. "I'm finished. I think it was the cookies that helped."

"Good," she said. "The rest are boxed up in the kitchen to bring to school, so if you want any more you're going to have to pay Hailey for them." She stood up and gave me a kiss on the top of my head. "Off to bed now!"

"Thanks, Mom. Thanks for everything. I love you."

"I love you too, sweetheart. Good night."

Even though it was late, I still followed all the good sleep hygiene stuff that I could. It couldn't hurt, right? I drifted off quickly (lots of practice lately) and hoped the article would be a hit.

★ ★ ★

"We made two thousand doll-ars! We made two thousand doll-ars!" Hailey was dancing around the cafeteria on Friday at lunch with a huge smile on her face.

"Hailey, that's awesome!" I cried, and I threw my arms around her and hugged her.

"Thanks! And thanks for your help and support!" she added. "Your cookies were great. I can't believe you had time to make so many!"

"Well . . ." I said, thinking of my mom slaving away in the kitchen. "It helps to have a nice mom."

"I'll thank her later when I come over for you to tutor me in language arts."

"Hailey!" I protested.

"Kidding!" She laughed. "But let's do something fun tonight, okay?"

"Okay."

"Oh, look! The paper!" Mr. Trigg was in the doorway of the cafeteria, handing out the fresh issues of the *Cherry Valley Voice*. This is always my favorite part of the journalism process: watching people read my work.

Hailey set off to get a copy.

"Bring me one!" I called after her, and she waved in acknowledgment.

Suddenly a voice behind me said, "How's it going, Sleepy?"

I jumped a little but then smiled. "You've got to stop sneaking up on people, Captain!" I said, turning around to see him.

Michael blushed. "Hey, cut that out!"

"Oooh, finally! A nickname that bugs *you*! This is my lucky day!"

All around me kids were starting to read the paper and the chatter was beginning. Hailey returned.

"Yo," she said to Michael.

"Yo," he said back.

"Anything good this issue?" I asked Hailey.

"Well, there's a front-page article by Sam Martone, with additional reporting by Michael Lawrence. But I'm reading Dear Know-It-All first, as usual!" said Hailey.

"A loyal customer," said Michael. I didn't dare look at him for fear he was implying she was loyal to me. I also didn't dare ask her if Know-It-All was better this week, because I didn't trust my voice not to betray me in some way. "Thanks for the credit. You didn't need to do that, you know."

I shrugged. "You earned it."

Suddenly Molly appeared. "Hailey! Know-It-All is awesome this week! Did you read it yet?"

"Reading it!" murmured Hailey.

Molly turned to me and said, "Sam, I loved your article. And, oh my gosh, I totally worship your sister! She is so awesome! She's telling me today where she got her boots so I can get some just like them!"

"Great!" I said. "Hailey will be so psyched to hear that news." Molly looked at me in confusion, and I had a little giggle.

Hailey snapped her paper shut. "I read it. What a relief!"

I had to laugh. "Why?"

"Know-It-All is back to his usual self. This was a great one. I thought he'd lost it, but he's back!"

"Maybe he got a good night's sleep," said Michael, nudging me with his elbow.

OMG, does Michael know?

I gulped and said, "Well, Know-It-All hasn't read my sleep article yet, so how could he have? Unless he worked on the sleep article *with me*?" It never hurts to cast suspicion elsewhere in these situations.

Michael laughed. "I wonder if he or she is so tired, he or she falls asleep in conference rooms?"

Okay, he totally knows! What to say? What to say? Act cool, Martone . . .

"Happens all the time," I said. "You'd be surprised, Captain."

Journalist Has the Last Word. Rejoices in Victory!

Extra! Extra!

Want the scoop on what Samantha is up to next?

Here's a sneak peek of the twelfth book in the Dear Know-It-All series:

Stop the Presses!

SPRING BREAK FAILS TO GARNER EXCITEMENT AT MARTONE HOUSEHOLD

Have you ever gotten up close and personal with a piece of paper? Like when you're writing a report for school, do you stop for a moment and hold the page up to the light, examining it in all its glorious papery beauty? Sometimes the paper shines so much that the words look like they're vibrating on the page. Sometimes it's so thin that you can almost see right through it and it's almost like a magic trick that there are words on the page.

But I've always loved to write—and read—but it wasn't until my date—er, field trip—to see our newspaper's print run with Michael Lawrence that I began to fully appreciate the unique beauty of the printed page. We took a tour of Flyprint, the company that prints the *Cherry Valley Voice*, and Mr. Dunleavy, our sales rep, showed us the enormous rolls of paper, the printing plates, and the presses in action. It was, like, the coolest thing ever. I mean, I love the rush of writing a story for the paper on a deadline but actually seeing the story being printed? Totally cool.

Since the trip, though, I've been looking around and noticing that not a lot of my friends seem to feel the same way I do about the whole paper experience. It seems like everyone's always wrapped up in some electronic device. Take my sister, Allie, for instance. Sometimes I'll be sitting in my room when I hear my phone chime and see that there's a text message from her. She is texting me from her bedroom, which is *right next to my bedroom.* Would it really be so difficult for her to walk across the hall and talk to me in person?

Allie isn't alone, though. I was reading a study (and I admit, I was reading it on my computer), and it said that 63 percent of teenagers use text messages to communicate with their friends every day. Meanwhile, only 35 percent said that they talk face-to-face with their friends outside of school on a daily basis.

You want to know what's even more tragic? I haven't heard from Michael Lawrence in five whole days. Not a face-to-face conversation, not a phone call, not even a "Hey, what's up, Pasty?" text. It's reaching crisis level, for sure.

I was kind of in a grouchy mood, since on top of my not seeing Michael, my mom suggested that Allie and I clean out our bedrooms. Allie and I don't have much in common except we both are kind of pack rats. I like to keep books, newspapers, and magazines. Allie likes to keep every bit of clothing she's ever worn. I'm not a happy camper. I like my room the way it is and I hate change. So you can see the problem.

I heard my mom rustling around in her room, so I decided to go and see what she was doing and maybe torture her a little by whining about how bored I was. But instead of finding her buried in a pile of receipts and bank statements, I caught her looking in a furniture catalog.

"What are you doing, Mom?" I asked.

"Oh, Sam, I'm glad you're here," Mom said. "I want to talk to you about the new bedroom project you and Allie have been working on. I know that cleaning out your rooms hasn't been fun for you two. So here's my proposal. I'm not going to be able to dig out from the pile of papers I've been buried under for a while. But once this project is finished, I'll have a lot more free time on my hands. And that's where these come in. . . ."

Mom opened up her night table, pulled out a stack of magazines, and spread them out on the bed. They were all glossy and printed on really beautiful paper (sorry, I just can't let it go)—magazines like *Elle Decor*, *House Beautiful*, and *Home and Design*.

"Are you giving me an assignment?" I asked. "Write an article about the horrors of cleaning your room to pitch to one of these magazines?"

"No, but that's not a bad idea, if you're up for it," Mom said. "I am giving you a different kind of assignment. It's a redesign partnership. These magazines are just a start. You and Allie should use them as a springboard to build a plan for redesigning your rooms. You know, cut out pictures of furniture you like, collect swatches of colors and patterns that we could use, stuff like that. When you've got a good idea of what you want, we'll work together after school and on the weekends to make it come to life."

"A new bedroom?" I cried. "Thanks, Mom. That would be awesome." I love my room, but it's probably time to get rid of the curtains that have little bows on them. I started thinking about bedrooms I've seen on TV or in the movies that were really cool and looked like you'd want your friends to hang out there with you. "So," I said, "do you think maybe in the next few months we could do this?"

Mom gave me a hug and kissed the top of my head.

"Oh, Sam, I'm sorry you've been at the mercy of my schedule," she said. "I really am. I promise it will be within the next month. First things first: Clean them out so we have a fresh space to work with. Maybe you and Allie can spend some time together this weekend working on this project.

You know, some big-sister-little-sister bonding?"

Hmm. I had to spend "quality time" with Allie? But I'd get a new bedroom in return. In the end I supposed it would be worth it.

check all the blogs and news websites
first thing every